NOON

PROLOGUE

The Lake

(2006)

वारिणो भिद्यमानस्य किमयं तुमुलो ध्वनिः
राघवस्य वचः श्रुत्वा कौतूहलसमन्वितम्
कथयामास धर्मात्मा तस्य शब्दस्य निश्चयम्
कैलासपर्वते राम मनसा निर्मितं सरः
ब्रह्मणा नरशार्दूल तेनेदं मानसं सरः

'"What is this tumultuous din of clashing waters?" Hearing Rághava's words, so expressive of his curiosity, the righteous sage explained the cause of that sound. "Rama, on Mount Kailása there is a lake that Brahma produced from his mind, *manas.* Because of this, tiger among men, it is called Lake Mánasa."'*

The Ramayana, Valmiki

* \skt{manas} n. mind (in its widest sense as applied to all the mental powers), intellect, intelligence, understanding, perception, sense, conscience, will [Lat. {miner-va}.]

On the day I met my father's family for the first time, a strange coincidence occurred on a train. It was October 2006, a year after the great earthquake in Kashmir. I was travelling south from that troubled region, when a young man burst into my cabin.

He wore flared jeans and a faded denim jacket. His long, well-brushed hair was tied back and there was something of the Frontier in his dark sunburned features. He gave me no explanation for barging in. He simply dropped into the facing seat, loosened the coloured bands of his ponytail, and began talking.

I felt I had to respond to this casual restlessness: 'The conductor will come. If he sees that you don't have the right ticket, he'll send you back or fine you.'

The intruder gazed fixedly at me, then smiled and extended his hand. 'Mirwaiz,' he said. 'When he comes, I will go back.'

'Rehan,' I replied, reluctantly taking his hand, 'Rehan Tabassum.'

'Where are you headed, Rehan?'

'La Mirage. And you?'

'Port bin Qasim.'

'Long trip,' I said, with the visitor's pride at working out these distances in an unfamiliar country. 'When will you get there?'

Mirwaiz looked out of the window, as if expecting the darkened landscape, dotted here and there with a well or granary bathed in fitful tube light, to give him an answer.

'In the morning,' he said. 'I'd say we're still in Punjab, still an hour or two from La Mirage.'

And, as if deciding this time had been given him to deepen his acquaintance with me, he began firing questions.

'Do you live in La Mirage?'

'No.'

'Why are you going there then?'

'To visit my family.'

'Do *they* live there?'

'Some.'

'Where?'

'In La Mirage.'

'I know, but where?'

'I'm not sure,' I lied.

Then eyeing the red threads on my wrist, he said: 'Are you Muslim?'

'Yes.'

'Why do you wear this string?'

'It's from a Sufi shrine,' I lied again.

'OK, and this bangle?'

'My grandmother gave it to me. She's a Sikh.'

'And your mother?'

The question took me away for a moment. My mind brought up the two women, one now dead, the other in another country. And from a perverse desire to simplify my life to a stranger on a train, I said, now lying extravagantly, 'She was a Sikh too, but became Muslim after marrying my father.'

'What does he do?'

'My father? Business,' I said uncertainly.

'What kind?'

'What's with all the questions!'

Mirwaiz's eyes grew wide with apology. He sat up and gestured towards the door.

I felt bad, felt I was playing up formalities, when really I was happy to talk. 'No, stay,' I said, 'I'm sorry. The answer to your question is that I don't really know. We don't speak.'

'Oh,' Mirwaiz said, with compassion. 'God willing you will again one day.'

I thought of correcting him, but he said, 'Still; good or bad, it is better to have a father than not. I had one. Once,' he added, enjoying the effect of his words. 'But now there is just my mother and sister.'

'I'm sorry. I didn't . . .'

'Don't worry,' Mirwaiz said, filling the silence quickly. Then, unprompted, he explained – using the English word – 'Earthquake.'

'Oh!' I managed, and unable to hold my curiosity, added, 'I heard, of course.'

'Hearing, saab, is one thing,' Mirwaiz replied, 'to see is another. My sister heard too, but she didn't see.' Then almost boastfully, he said, 'I *saw* it all, I saw the Jhelum disappear.'

He began, in a sawing movement, to rub his palm over his chest.

'Our village was one of those typical villages of the Jhelum Valley. Mud houses, slate roofs. Dark hills, river below. A pukka government school. One mobile phone tower. That's about it. I could see it all very clearly that day. I had taken the herd out to one of the surrounding mountains from where everything was visible. October's a good month in the hills. Bright sunshine, cool breezes, great vistas. The goats were happy too. Mast! Eating grass. It was just like any other day.'

He paused, seemed to size me up and continued:

'I was half-dozing in the sunshine, my eyes resting on Madhu, when all of a sudden, saab, she jumped! Three whole feet from where she stood. A stationary goat just thrown from the earth. I'd never seen anything like it in my life. And no sooner had her hooves struck the ground below than she lost her footing and began to roll. I leapt up and tried catching her, but was too late. She was lost, Rehan saab. In seconds, she was tumbling down the hill, hitting against it, legs splayed, trying desperately to regain her footing, bleating with fear. I couldn't make out where she had fallen. Because at that precise moment, my eyes were drawn back to the others, all now jumping, all slipping and falling.

'That was when it came, Rehan saab, that was when the noise came. The movie had been on mute until then. Don't believe people when they say it sounds like dynamite or an avalanche. I've heard those things; this is not like that. When it comes, you know, in your gut, that only creation itself would dare make a sound like that. I heard it travel, Rehan saab, I heard the actual tearing of the earth. It rode through the valley, like the waters of a burst dam.

'Then just before everything went dark, I got a glimpse of the gorge. The goats were specks flying headlong down the mountainside into what I thought was the Jhelum. But where was the Jhelum? When I looked down I saw that there was almost nothing left of the river. Its mighty expanse, before my eyes, was slowing, and turning to a trickle. Then, as water is sucked into a drain, I saw it swallowed up by the ground. My last memory was of its empty bed, a nest of white glistening eggs!

'Around me, the forest had emptied. No birds, no animals. Even the earth had turned out her inhabitants. The forest floor swarmed with creatures we never normally saw, worms, red ants, snakes, pouring out of holes in the ground.'

'And your family . . . ?' I said with alarm.

Mirwaiz gazed strangely at me, as if considering the nature of my curiosity.

'I'll tell you how I found them,' he said at last. 'It was afternoon when finally I was able to make my way back home. We lived a few miles from the village in a house, to which my father had recently added a storeroom. We used it, you know, for this and that, bicycles and bed linen. So, anyway, I arrived back at the house to find that though it had been severed from its base, the actual structure had survived. And so, too, would have anyone who had been inside it. But that – and, saab, such was his ill-fortune! – was not where my father had been when . . .'

'The storeroom?' I said.

Mirwaiz nodded. 'All its walls had come down, but the doorway still stood. I looked inside and, at first, I didn't see him. But just as I was turning away, my eyes landed on his small bloated face. It was covered in white cement dust, and but for a bit of dried blood at the corner of the mouth, it was peaceful. Saab, like a child asleep, down to the blankets and sheets. Just one thing was off: ants. Ants everywhere,' Mirwaiz said with a shudder.

'I dusted the cement from his face, and with my own spit, wiped the blood from his mouth. I tried pulling his body out from under the stone shelves, but couldn't move it. Then from behind, I heard my mother's voice. Her face was also covered in dust and her clothes spattered with blood. She saw my father and moaned, "Hai! You too! He's taken you too."

'Note the words, saab: "He's taken you too." My mother, you see, could trust everything to her God. He had sent this upon us as punishment and the ones who survived were punished most. But I could not feel this way. I just felt very quiet and alone. Free almost, free of all my ties. God? God hota, toh He would have at least let us give my father a decent burial.

'Or perhaps He decreed otherwise. For after the earthquake He sent rain. And it rained, saab, as it has never rained in the Jhelum Valley. We had with great difficulty, inch by inch, and with the help of an iron beam, retrieved my father's body. I had washed and prepared it for proper burial, then, using a small pick and my bare hands, dug him a grave. There was no one to administer the rites, of course. But the beauty of our religion is that for all the major occasions – birth, death and marriage – a priest is not needed. Any good Muslim can perform the rites.

'The grave, saab, had not been ready ten minutes when darkness and rain came at once. The bed of the Jhelum flashed, like a live wire, and, in seconds, the little makeshift grave into which my mother had thrown some rose petals and coins filled with muddy water; its outlines crumbled and were washed away. The mountains, with nothing to hold the soil together, began to run into the river. We had to clutch, saab, with all our strength to my father's body to stop it from joining that downward flow of rocks and earth. His shroud, a normal bed sheet, was drenched and dirtied. But we dared not go inside the house, Rehan saab, we dared not go inside the house. We sat there, like that only, all night, clutching his body till dawn, unable to give it burial or shelter.'

Mirwaiz's voice faded before the sudden airy thump of a second train. For a moment the lights of the carriage dimmed. In the darkness, it occurred to me that the events he described had happened a year ago to the date almost. He had obviously just been back. Why?

The question brought a twist of a smile to his face.

'I'll tell you, I'll tell you. You see after it happened, we were separated, my mother and I, from my sister, and not reunited till many days later when we were brought to the Tabassum relief camp. You know those Qasimic Call people, telephone company *walleh*? Mr Narses . . .'

And here was the coincidence. 'Mirwaiz,' I muttered, unable to hold my surprise, 'I don't just know them; they're my family. Narses is my father's brother-in-law.'

Mirwaiz was impressed. 'Mr Narses? Your uncle?' he said. 'So you are of those Tabassums. I didn't realize when you gave me your name. Sahil Tabassum, then, must be your father?'

'Yes,' I said unsurely.

'By God, I knew there was a reason why I felt myself drawn to your cabin tonight. Fate, you see, Rehan saab, fate.'

He let the wonder of it linger a moment longer, then abruptly resumed his account.

'I began by telling you that I had seen; and so had my mother; but my sister, saab, had not. She was in another part of the valley when all this happened; and this made it very hard for her to digest. Ever since we moved to the plains, she's been haunted by how unreal it all feels. She keeps saying she needs some way to remember. "To fill the hole in her life. Anything," she repeats, "anything, Mirwaiz. I don't care if it's just a picture of flattened houses; I need something."

'That was why I went back, saab, on the one-year anniversary. She was to have come too but, in the end, she backed out. Which is good, for she would not have been able to handle what I found.'

'What did you find?'

Mirwaiz raised himself up and removed a mobile phone from the pocket of his jeans. He brought up an image on its screen, which he looked at, before handing the phone to me.

On the small screen, I was able only to make out a blue lake in bright sunshine, a line of trees in autumn colours and, in the distance, the snows of the high mountains.

'I don't understand.'

'Look closely,' Mirwaiz said, his dark features intent. Then taking the phone back for a second, he zoomed in on what was a tiny elevation on the glassy surface of the lake, a point of orange and white on its wide expanse, no more prominent than a buoy.

'What is that?'

'The top of our mobile phone tower! The Qasimic Call tower, put there by your family!' Mirwaiz replied, almost laughing. 'It is our one memorial to what happened. For to stop the Jhelum, Rehan saab, is no small thing!'

Seeing that he had restored my faith in him, he took on a different tone.

'So, you see, Rehan saab, when a man sees what I've seen, this lake now in place of our lives, and the violence that made it, he does not want to think too much; he just wants to live as he wouldn't mind dying, no regrets, king size! What do you say?'

The train pulled into La Mirage. An evening scene of porters in orange and food-sellers greeted us. Still feeling the force of Mirwaiz's story, I rose to get my bags. As I was leaving the cabin, I paused in the doorway. The light coming in through a grilled window left a jaundiced imprint on Mirwaiz's handsome face. He was looking up at me expectantly.

'Rehan saab. Your father is a very big man. So is his son, Isphandiyar Tabassum, and his brother-in-law, Mr Narses. They have many companies. See if you can't speak to one of them about a job for me in Port bin Qasim?'

'I'll try, Mirwaiz,' I replied. 'I'll definitely try. But I can't promise anything. You see,' I added, looking long at him one last time, 'our situations are not so different. Sahil Tabassum may be my father, but I've never met him.'

1

Last Rites

(1989)

'We passionately long for there to be another life in which we shall be similar to what we are here below. But we do not pause to reflect that, even without waiting for that other life, in this life, after a few years, we are unfaithful to what we once were, to what we wished to remain immortally.'

Remembrance of Things Past, Marcel Proust

The dressing table was the first thing she had bought herself since Sahil. It had attracted her, with its tiny bulbs, gilt and mirrors, from the pages of a foreign magazine. She decided at length to take the magazine down to the colony market and have the dressing table copied. Rati Ram, the carpenter, inspected it, seemed to translate its charms into an Indian reality, then agreed to reproduce it for a few hundred rupees. When he returned a few days later with his replica, thickly coated in gold paint, and decorated with fat full-sized bulbs and crudely cut strips of mirror, its arrival caused tension in the little house with the gardenia tree.

'Phansy shmansy,' her mother sniffed, as the men brought it in.

'Give me a break, Mama. You know very well I haven't so much as bought myself a salwar since I moved here. And it's not as if you're paying for it.'

'Who's saying I am! But let me remind you, I pay for other things. And they cost me an arm and a leg. Not that I'm not happy to do it. But I won't have you getting on your high horse.'

'Would you like me to thank you for it again? "Thank you, Mama, for paying Rehan's fees; I am eternally grateful and so is he." Happy?'

'Don't take that tone with me. He's my grandson. I'll give him what I like. I don't need you to thank me.'

Rehan looked into the house from the veranda, where moments before he had been servicing his gods, cleaning the idols, putting fresh marigolds in their tray. When he heard the raised voices, he slipped behind the cooler. Through its grey slats, the two women appeared to him as mute shadows, their voices drowned out by the whirr of the cooler's fan and the slurping of its pipes. He saw his mother pace and bring her palms together in frustration. His grandmother, in reply, threw up her arms and rushed out of the room, leaving Udaya alone. Rehan's gaze was diverted by drops of water growing fat along the cooler's soaked matting. They swelled, their bellies striped by the blaze. Then they fell fast and soundless to the few inches of dark water below. The room now was empty and a batch of fresh drops sprouted on the matting. Rehan returned to his gods.

Udaya had brought him to her mother's house as a temporary step after Sahil.

It had been impossible, once that relationship ended, to stay on in London. Not without Sahil. Who, after moving them out of his flat on Flood Street, became difficult and unreachable. He had always travelled a lot, between La Mirage, Dubai and London, and in the end, like an airline reducing its flights to a destination, he had come to London less and less. It had always only been an 'arrangement' forged fast when she became pregnant with Rehan. She had hung on to the hope that it would deepen. But after a last holiday in Kathmandu, to which Sahil brought along two children he claimed were his nephew and niece, the calls and visits came to an end.

Love was one reason she hung on in London; pride another. After the scandal of her relationship, she found it difficult to face her mother with the news that it was over, not three years after it had begun. She found work as a freelance lawyer, but made only enough to pay the rent on the north London bedsit they had moved into.

Then, several years after her last conversation with

Sahil, she ran into an uncle, visiting from Delhi. It was a bleak moment; she had been forced to sell some jewellery the day before; in her weakness, she confessed everything. He convinced her to let him prepare the ground with her mother and a few weeks later Udaya returned, with Rehan, to rebuild her life in the city she had left some years before, trusting completely to passion.

It had made sense at first to stay with her mother. But no sooner had she arrived than the fights began. And, as with those of her childhood, they seemed never to be about what they were ostensibly about. If then the issue of cutting her hair or smoking or marriage had become an expression of some deeper tension between them, so, now too, seemingly innocuous things, such as the cleanliness of the kitchen, the trouble in Punjab and Rehan's upbringing became laden with their old animus. The difference was that they were not alone. Rehan, every day more aware, was there among them; and she was determined to save him the scenes. It had been fight enough to convince her mother to let Rehan feed himself. Udaya had a secret terror that her mother, well-intentioned as it might be, would instil in him, through that special brand of Indian compassion that debilitates when it means to commiserate, a feeling of want or misfortune. Rehan had given no indication of ever being aware of Sahil's absence; and though she had given him his father's name and even an explanation of a kind – *Sometimes, just as you fight with your friends, grown-ups fight too* – he had never seemed interested in knowing more. It made her happy to think of him as unscathed by their separation.

No, if she was to protect Rehan, she must find her own place, and quickly. She had already begun making enquiries.

* * *

From where he lay on the bed, Rehan could see just his mother's back, her long straight hair and a few inches of flesh trapped between her petticoat and blouse. She sat before the new dressing table, opening her mouth wide for lipstick, smacking her lips closed on a tissue and reaching for tweezers to remove stray hairs.

'Where are you going for dinner?' Rehan asked.

'It's a work dinner, baba. A client . . .'

'What's his name?'

'Amit, Amit Sethia.'

'What does he do?'

'He's an industrialist.'

'What's an industrialist?'

'Someone with industries. Coal, steel etc. . . .'

'Is he rich?'

'Yes, baba,' Udaya said, closing one eye over a silver stick lined with kohl.

'Ma,' Rehan said abruptly, 'why do you hate Nani?' His mother blinked rapidly, half-turning around. An expression of withheld amusement and a threat to come clean played on her face.

'Rehan! What have you heard?'

'Nothing, Ma, really. I swear. I was just curious.'

'Why are you suddenly asking me if I hate your grandmother?'

'You both fight a lot so I was just wondering.'

Turning back to the mirror, but watching him closely with one kohled eye, she said, 'Well, it's not that I hate Nani, it's just that there comes a point in everyone's life when they stop seeing their mother or father as just their mother and father but as people. And sometimes you like those people for who they are, and sometimes you find, well, that you don't have much in common with them. Nani and I, for instance, have never had much in common. She didn't understand me; I couldn't understand her. We were miles apart. She believed in God and couldn't believe she'd produced a daughter who didn't.

I couldn't believe she believed in a God who cared how long your hair was. I mean was this God a hairdresser?'

Rehan laughed loudly. He didn't mind her insulting her own Sikh god as long as she didn't begin on the Hindu ones, for which he had acquired an unlikely obsession since his arrival in India.

'She read Mills and Boons,' his mother continued, 'I didn't. She was forever concerned about respectability; I couldn't care less. When your aunt got married, she told me, "Now, it's too late for you. I've told your father to put some money aside, and bas, try and best make do." I was twenty-five! No, she was horrible!' Udaya, now nearly fully made up, smiled as she spoke and it seemed to drain her words of ill feeling. Rehan adored his grandmother, and it was unsettling that his mother, whose voice was like the voice of truth, could feel differently. He hated to be at odds with her. But whenever he tried to bring her around to his way of thinking, she would irritate him by taking an agree-to-disagree tone.

'I love Nani!' he said provocatively. 'And when her ship comes in, she's going to buy me Castle Grayskull for my gods to live in.'

'So you must,' his mother replied, reflecting on whether Rehan had been told what his grandmother's ship coming in would mean. 'She's been wonderful to you.'

'Stop talking in that fake voice!' Rehan yelled.

His mother smiled and turned her full attention to putting on her sari. She chose a handbag and, carefully, the things that went in it – all of which angered Rehan so much that he stormed out.

Summer power cuts and fluctuations had begun and the light in the corridor was dim. The disc-shaped ceiling light, high above like a white Frisbee, grew fainter and fainter, till its milky glass barely sustained a glow. Then like a small angry sun burning away a thick bank of clouds, it flared, sending Rehan fleeing down the stairs that separated his grandmother's section of the house from his mother's. Below, where the surge had ended and the light was dull and dusty again, servants were setting the table, lighting the odd white candle. Rehan slipped past his grandmother's room in the hope of beginning his favourite mythical movie, *The Marriage of Shiva and Parvati*, before dinner.

He had only been watching a few minutes when he heard his grandmother call him.

'No, no, Nani, please. Not now, just come here and see where we are.'

She wandered in a second later, wearing a loose, faded salwar kameez. Her greying hair was in a thin plait and when she sat down next to Rehan, he could smell Nivea cream on her. Her skin was smooth and her eyes, though losing colour, still shone. There was something coquettish about her smile of clean-capped teeth, giving, even now, the impression of a once-beautiful woman. Rehan grabbed her soft stomach and squeezed it. She pretended at first to be indifferent to the drama coming from the old Japanese VCR, but Rehan knew she was riveted. The story had raced ahead and Parvati, witnessing her father dishonour her husband, a bellied and middle-aged Shiva, was about to commit herself to the sacrificial fire.

Rehan's grandmother watched through her large amber-rimmed spectacles, the glare exposing fingerprints on their lenses, as Parvati's anger built. She clutched an optician's artificial leather case in her hands, and muttered, 'OK then, why not! Arre, suno!' she yelled for a servant. 'Koi hai?'

Bihari arrived a moment later, a stained napkin draped over his shoulder.

'Bihari, go and get baba's food.' Then, she added, 'And listen, don't say anything to Udaya madam.'

'Nani, yes!' Rehan squealed.

'Your mother will kill us.'

'No, no, she'll be fine. She's going out to dinner at the house of a rich industrist.'

'Industrialist, baba.'

Parvati, burning with rage, was moments away from committing the first sati ever when dinner arrived on a steel and tinted glass trolley.

'Baba, come on now, eat your food.'

'Nani, please, just see where we are. Please feed me.'

'Your mother will throw a fit. She has told me time and time again not to feed you.'

'Come on, Nani, what difference does it make? Look, look, Shiva's being told about Parvati having jumped in the fire.'

Drum rolls had begun in Kailash, demons tittered and studio lightning flashed as Shiva was informed of Parvati's fate.

'He's going to dance the tandav,' Rehan's grand-mother gasped, 'he is the Natraj after all.' And this simple comment on the drama, said in a voice fearful and resigned, as if his grandmother, too, was part of the world Shiva was to destroy, spread gooseflesh over Rehan's arms and back.

'Nani!' he breathed. She put a little packet of food, mutton and lentils in his mouth. He chewed tensely, as Shiva now bent over Parvati's ashes, fingered them gently as though searching for some small trinket. Rehan found this scene, of the most powerful god in the universe grieving, very affecting. Shiva's loneliness was so acute; it made Rehan wish that they were friends so that he could help lessen it in some way. At the same time the display of male emotion intrigued him.

'Nani, look how he's almost crying.'

'He's sad, no?' Rehan's grandmother said, putting another bite of food in his mouth. She tried another but Rehan turned his face away.

'But still strong, Nani?'

'Yes, baba. Eat. One for Nani . . .'

He accepted.

'One for Mama . . .'

'No, Nani, enough.'

'One for Shiva ji.'

'Nani!'

Then it occurred to Rehan to ask why Parvati had jumped into the fire in the first place. His grandmother smiled knowingly. 'Baba Re,' she said in a hushed voice, 'the supreme sacrifice.' And perhaps thinking the words too complicated for a child, she added, 'When a girl enters her husband's house, his honour becomes hers. Then everything else becomes secondary, even her own parents' house, which once she leaves it for her husband's, is no longer hers.'

Distracted by their conversation and the noise from the television, neither of them heard the clatter of Udaya's heels. His grandmother was still trying to shove in a last mouthful when Rehan saw her standing in the doorway in her mustard chiffon sari. Her long black hair was washed and dried, the evening bag hung from her arm and her dark skin was touched with rouge and brownish red lipstick. Taking in the scene before her, Udaya's smile fled.

'Mama!' she moaned. 'What are you doing?'

Rehan's grandmother pursed her lips; a martyred expression formed on her face; she looked directly ahead at the television, where Vishnu had now persuaded Shakti to stand between Shiva and the destruction of the world. 'The next step you take,' Shakti said, looking up with simpering resolve at the dancing Shiva, 'will be on my head.' Rehan stared at his mother as though she had jumped out of the screen.

'Mama, how many times am I to tell you he is too old to be fed! If at this age he can't feed himself, we may as well institutionalize him.'

His grandmother glanced sideways at Rehan. He sputtered, 'Ma, it was me. I asked Nani to feed me.'

She looked up at Udaya with satisfaction.

'Shut up, you're a child. You don't make these decisions. I, as your mother, am telling you that you will feed yourself.' Then, as if addressing her in another language, Udaya said to her mother: 'And, Mama, cut it out. I know what you're doing. I've made my decision but, in the meantime, I will not have you retard this child with your religious crap.'

Her anger spent, Udaya looked tenderly at Rehan.

'Anyway I'm off to dinner. Go to bed soon, baba.'

With this, she turned around and strode out of the house, leaving a trail of perfume to settle over the smell of food. Rehan jumped up, and putting a conciliatory hand on his grandmother's knee, trotted out after his mother.

He caught her at the end of the cement drive, where, in a small patch of lawn, with a thin grass cover, bare earth showing through in places, there were beds of dahlias with scraggly manes. It was here, almost magically, that amid the drabness of the house and the malnourished plants, a rare gardenia flourished. The tree had a knotted trunk with a slender curve that brought its canopy of fleshy leaves to the centre of the garden. Deep within each cluster, like shallow wells of moonlight, grew white scented flowers, as heavy as fruit.

The gardenia was another point of tension between mother and daughter. It had come with the house, but Rehan's grandmother hated the tree, accusing it of steal-ing light from the other plants. Udaya thought it beautiful

and suspected that the real cause for her mother's antipathy was the tree's bewitching aspect, its poison and
femininity. She had convinced Rehan that it was really a
rakshasa, waiting to reveal its true form when the moment
was right.

Rehan made out his mother standing near the Suzuki
in the light of a single caged bulb.

'Ma, Ma, wait.'

'Baba, why are you barefoot?'

He looked down at his feet, felt he was losing critical
amounts of goodwill, but pattered on regardless.

'Ma, sorry, I'll put some slippers on. I just have to
tell you something,' he said, approaching quickly. He felt
his mother much bigger in her heels, her head lost to
some dark summit.

'Listen, Ma,' he said, taking the adult tone of voice
she often adopted with him, 'I understood what you just
said to Nani. I know what the "decision" is; but I don't
think we should do it; I don't think we should move.'

Udaya came suddenly out of shadow and Rehan was
struck by how beautiful and strong she seemed. She gave
him the special look she used when they were having a
private joke.

'Baba,' she said, 'I've seen a very nice flat and believe
me, you'll love it. You'll have your own room. Your

own bed. You can have your friends over whenever you want and Nani won't be far, but we must have our own place.'

The idea of the flat filled Rehan with unease. He hated the thought of being in some other part of town, separated from his grandmother. But in speaking of it to him as a secret undertaking, his mother won him over for the time being. He felt it important not to let her down. He waited till the Suzuki's red brake lights had disappeared down the still and silent street, then went back inside.

The next day, when the sun blazed and the white edges of the city's pavements throbbed, Udaya received an unexpected call from Rehan's school. She had been in her own thoughts all morning, recalling impressions from the night before. It had been a beautiful party; there had been many journalists and politicians, a handful of diplomats. The French ambassador, Servain, had expressed a special interest in the meaning of her name. 'Dawn?' he asked, holding her hand as he spoke. 'No,' she had replied, 'of the dawn, I believe.' 'Udaya, udaya,' he muttered softly to himself, 'not dawn, but of the dawn.' Udaya flushed with embarrassment.

They were interrupted by their host. 'Enough, you

dirty old dip,' he had said, only half-jokingly, it seemed, 'keep to your own women. I invited this lovely lady so that *I* could speak to her.' Amit Sethia had a brash, clumsy style, Udaya had thought at the time, but she was flattered by the attention he paid her. After the upheavals of the past few years, there was something exciting about being out and about again, desirable to men. It felt like the return of normal life.

The voice on the other end of the phone was too frazzled to explain why she wanted Udaya to come in person to pick Rehan up from school; she couldn't say what the matter was. He was safe; 'there was no cause to worry'; but he outright refused to leave and was insisting that his mother come to fetch him. He had never done anything like this before, never even been homesick. And Udaya, sliding the Suzuki's keys off her glass-topped desk, had a feeling of dread.

The road in front of the British School was crowded when she arrived. The imported embassy cars made a barrier of sorts, their shapes smooth, their gleam hard. Her own car windows were thrown open as if in distress, and as she could find no place to park, she stopped in front of the school gate, trying to spot Rehan through gaps in the glittering wall of steel and tinted glass. At last, raising herself up on the car floor, she caught sight of him over the white caps of chauffeurs. Rehan ran out to her, his brown water bottle banging against his thighs. Bolting past the line of cars, he made her heart race. The next thing she knew he had jumped into the seat next to her, which he was not allowed to do.

It was Rehan's first time in the front and Udaya insisted that he wear a seat belt. Suzuki had been the first to introduce them in India, but they didn't seem very secure: the grey belt, clinging to a thin strip of exposed green metal, hung loosely around her son. The car felt light, too light; it felt tinny and destructible. Udaya had bought it in part from money lent her by her mother and in part through a system of monthly instalments, which she always brought up when Rehan asked for something expensive.

'Ma, can we turn the AC on?'

'No, baba, you know we can't. Don't you remember what happened the last time we did?'

'The engine started to cough?'

'Yes.'

He had told her to buy the model with in-built air conditioning, but she had felt it was too much. His grandmother had said to buy the cheaper car and install the air conditioner later. But the heavy machine that hung from the car's dashboard put too much strain on the engine. And so, the AC remained off, its blue and orange lights unlit, its wide black grill mute, the dark gaps, like cartoon teeth, grinning impotently.

The heat was terrible. The Suzuki's plastic seats softened, the short shadows of trees shrank from the day, Rehan pulled at his seat belt. Which after being violently extended, only partially returned to its original position.

'Don't, baba.'

'But it's hot!'

'I know, but if you do that, you'll have to sit in the back. Do you want to sit in the back?'

'No.'

'Then sit properly and don't pull off the seat belt. It's to keep you safe.'

'But what if the car is going to explode and I need to run away?'

'It's not going to explode . . .'

'If!'

'Then you open the belt and run away.'

'If I have to run away quickly?'

'Then you open the belt quickly and run away.'

Rehan, enjoying his mother's fluency, chuckled. 'But what if I need to jump out of the window?'

'Rehan!' And his name said in this tone, under these circumstances, contained a threat. Rehan gauged it well.

He seemed to be about to speak, but then looking out on the day, itself an element of his fear, he became quiet.

'What, baba?' Udaya prodded him gently.

They passed a blue ice-cream cart on the side of the road. A man with an open shirt and a small, bird-like chest lay asleep on its cool aluminium surface.

'Ma, can I have a chocolate bonanza?'

'Baba, now? Really? The man's asleep.'

Rehan looked at her with a stern expression, as if appalled that she could mistake his genuine need for child-ish whim. She pulled over the car and honked her horn. The man rose drunkenly and came over to the window. Rehan waited patiently for the transparent plastic cup, through which it was possible to see a swirl of real choc-olate coiled many times about itself. The cup had a lid that fitted neatly into its bottom, making a stand of sorts, and in Rehan's mind, spoke of a special imported elegance.

A spoon or two in, he began: 'The twins' grandmother is dead.' The twins were his best friends in school.

'O, baba! I'm so sorry,' Udaya said, though not quite sure why the death of this apparent stranger should have so unnerved her son.

Rehan, sensing something false in his mother's tone, added: 'She was murdered. In a flat!'

'Oh, God,' Udaya said, wanting to shield him from his own news.

Rehan began to describe the afternoon scene of the old woman asleep; the doorbell ringing; her rising to open the front door. Then he couldn't go on. Something too vivid, too jarring had seized him. Udaya, through his sobs, couldn't understand the rest of what he said — doorbells and door eyes, broken chains, men in leather jackets, money taken or not taken.

It was only later that evening when she reached home and called the twins' mother that she was able to learn more. The old lady had lived alone in a flat in south Delhi and had been murdered by a man wearing a leather jacket. They knew this because he had tied up the maid, but spared her life; and yes, it was strange that he took no money. But the twins' mother was less mystified than Rehan by this: she felt he might have got scared and in a panic killed her mother-in-law and fled the scene.

They were due to move in a few weeks, but Rehan now would not hear of it. His opposition became so violent Udaya couldn't even persuade him to see the place she had found. She decided at last to show it to him by subterfuge.

One Saturday morning, soon after the rains arrived,

and Delhi's roads glistened and steamed, she offered to take him for a drive. On the way she said she wanted to stop at a friend's place.

'Why?'

'Just, to see what it's like and to pick something up.'

But Rehan was not so easily fooled.

'We're going to the flat, aren't we?'

'Yes.'

'OK,' he said, confirming his decision with a sigh. 'OK. Let's go.'

The barsati of 187 Golf Links overlooked a garden, now sodden with rainwater. A dim staircase, smelling of food and damp, served all the flats. Rehan and his mother climbed to the top and came to a white painted door.

Expecting to enter a closed space, Rehan let out a gasp when the door opened onto grey skies and a light monsoon breeze. At the centre of a vast terrace, there was a cottage of sorts bounded in with potted plants. Rehan's face lit up.

'See, baba! I told you that you'd like it.'

And he did. Walking through the room that would be his, shown a place where he would have his first bed – a bunk bed, his mother promised, where school friends could come and sleep over – Rehan reached for his mother's hand. They passed a recess in the wall and he could not resist trying it out for his gods. He let go of Udaya's hand and wandered up to the alcove, placing an action figure in it. And she, like an estate agent assured of her client's intentions, left his side for a moment and went to speak to the landlord.

For some seconds after she was gone, Rehan was fine, the magic of the place still working on him. Then looking around, he became aware of her absence. His gaze fastened on the judas in the front door, and he was conscious now of an awful daytime quiet, without the comforting din of Nani and her servants. Rehan decided to face his fear. He stood on his toes and peered through the door eye. At first he was cool as a man looking down the barrel of a shotgun, but when he saw the world become remote and threatening, through its cold lens, he began to lose his nerve.

There was something so unprotected about this flat. The limp chain between the door and frame that could so easily be axed away; the neighbours who could hear and be heard, and yet pretend not to have seen when it counted; and yes the judas planted in the door suggesting security, but through whose dwarfing lens murderers and tradesmen would appear alike.

When Udaya returned, she found Rehan transformed. Staring at her, he said, in a tone borrowed from his grandmother: 'But, Ma, aren't you worried what people will say about a woman living alone?'

Udaya laughed, making him angrier still. 'You've been spending too much time with your nani.'

'She's right, you know. People could say you're a keep.'

'A keep? A keep!'

She took hold of him by the wrist, as if to give him a tight slap, then without saying a word more, dragged him down the humid stairs.

When they arrived back at the house, Udaya, wishing to speak to her mother, was surprised to find her in a meeting. This was strange, not only because it was Saturday, but because she had never had any meetings before, especially not with men in suits, and trays laden with jalebis and samosas. Udaya recognized one of the visitors as Mr Cicada, the accountant. The other was an elderly gentleman with a stern moustache and a margin of fine white hair bordering the shiny expanse of his head.

'Kailash Nath ji,' Udaya's mother said piously, 'meet my daughter and grandson.'

The elderly man smiled into his moustache, bowing slightly.

Udaya, recognizing the name as that of a famous Delhi

contractor, was forced to swallow her anger and return the greeting.

Her mother, in the meantime, smiled knowingly at Rehan and gestured to a large box wrapped in garish paper.

'Nani,' Rehan gasped.

'Yes, baba Re, it has come in. My ship has come in.'

Rehan tore open the parcel and was within seconds moving his pantheon of gods, which till then had sat on a ledge near the cooler, into the plastic ramparts of Castle Grayskull.

The subject of the flat was dropped for the moment.

* * *

The rains were the worst Delhi had seen in a decade. They sent children dancing through puddles, they brought out black umbrellas and bicycles, they flooded underpasses; the Suzuki was stranded; Rehan floated paper boats in protest outside the house and tortured earthworms. He had apologized to his mother, but he still refused to move to the flat.

He had also become obsessed with the newspaper's coverage of the twins' grandmother's murder. He could only read slowly; and, eventually, tiring of the story's text, he would focus on the grainy, black and white images of the apartment block the old lady had lived in. *The Times of India* printed the image of the narrow, four-storey building – not unlike the one Udaya had shown Rehan – over and over again. The sight of it in bright sunlight, its entrances and windows black, never failed to chill him. He began to have terrible dreams.

One night, his mother was a mad Medusa with floating hair riding in the back of a jeep with a strange man. In another she was the girlfriend of the man in the leather jacket, plotting the old woman's murder. Rehan would wake up in the bed next to her, crying and gasping, recounting his dream as quickly as possible so that she could defuse it.

Udaya, watching him in this state, caught between nightmares and fixations, became convinced that his fears had other depths. In Delhi, in those days, on the cusp of change, child psychiatry was a rare thing, and it carried a stigma. But the dreams became so violent, the obsessions so unrelenting, that she began asking around.

* * *

Rehan had gone to the birthday party of his friend Karim Javeri. The Javeris were a rich Muslim family with a large house in Malcha Marg. When Udaya drove up to pick him up, she was met at the gate by Mrs Javeri, dressed in an embroidered cream kurta. Rehan was still playing inside and Mrs Javeri asked Udaya if she might have a word in private.

'Mrs Tabassum, I hope you don't mind . . .'

'Just Udaya is fine.'

'Udaya, I hope you don't mind my talking to you about this. It's a very small thing, but I thought you should know.'

'Not at all. Please go ahead, Mrs Javeri.'

'Naseem is fine.'

'Naseem.'

'Well, the thing is that we were all sitting, us adults, my husband, Sahil, and a few of our friends, inside the drawing room a moment ago. The cake had been cut; the children had finished their games, passing the parcel and what not; some were taking rides on the eli, others opening return presents, when your boy, Rehan – a sweet boy; one of Karim's very dear friends – came up to where we were sitting. He didn't say anything, or do anything . . .' Here, Mrs Javeri became flustered. 'I mean, he wasn't rude. He just stood there for a few seconds, quietly, till one of us took notice of him. And then he said, straight out of the blue, to my husband:

"You are not, by any chance . . ." These were his exact words – "Sahil, my father?"

'That was it. Nothing else. Nothing untoward. Just this. And when my husband, a little surprised naturally, said, "No, son, I'm not," he turned around and walked away. A small thing, Udaya, you know, but still, I felt if I was the mother, I should like to be informed. I hope you don't mind my . . .'

'No, no, Mrs Javeri, not at all. Thank you for telling me,' Udaya said, trying her best to appear calm. But, inside, she felt a kind of wonder at the changes taking place in her son, at the inscrutable logic of his fear.

On the way home, Udaya and Rehan hardly spoke. The light, after months of haze, had acquired sharpness and length. A cool, faintly scented wind was blowing. It was nearly Dussehra.

Gently Udaya mentioned what had occurred at the birthday party. 'You didn't really believe he was your father, did you?'

'No,' Rehan replied, and became quiet.

'Would you like to meet him, your father?' Udaya asked.

Rehan was silent for a moment, then said: 'Maybe, but not now.'

'I can write to him, you know. But, baba, I can't guarantee he will respond as you want him to.'

Rehan nodded.

'Baba, tell me: are you still scared?'

'No,' Rehan replied.

'What did you think, that just because she didn't have a man protecting her, something would happen to your mama?'

Rehan did not reply.

'I have you,' she said, 'and I'm a tough old thing myself. We'll be fine, believe me.'

They had crossed the flyover, and the Delhi that lay about them now was a city in which the fading afternoon, with colonial police stations and Muslim tombs in its fold, brought a kind of peace upon the passengers of the green Suzuki.

Rehan said, as if seeing a line of reason to its end, 'You think I'll ever meet him?'

'I'm sure you will,' his mother said, her strong and natural voice returning, 'and maybe you'll like him; or, as with Nani and me, maybe you'll want to meet him and move on. But whatever the case, give him a kick from your old mummy when you do.'

Rehan chuckled. 'Why, Ma?'

'Because,' she said, 'he was not very generous with either you or me.'

'He didn't give us anything? No car, no house?'

'Not a tissue to wipe my nose on.'

That was all that was said. It gave Rehan a great feeling of comfort, as if he had been made a partner in the life his mother had cobbled together for them. And though, in some important way, the fear of the last many months had already evaporated, what might have taken weeks or months to bear fruit was speeded to its conclusion by the scene they returned to that evening at the little house.

They arrived to find that a large blue and white board had gone up on its boundary wall. It read: Kailash Nath Sons and Associates. And just behind it, in the garden, a great commotion was underway. A gang of barefoot men in checked lungis and fraying vests tore up the lawn. The grass was gone; so were the flower beds and dahlias; all that remained standing, like a single tree over a fallow field, was the gardenia. Udaya and Rehan watched from inside the car as two men caught hold of its branches with a rope, pulling the canopy to the ground, while two others hacked away at the trunk, making white gashes. The tree seemed startled by the violence applied to it.

The gashes multiplied and it fell within minutes, not with a crash but a swoon, still holding aloft its many flowers. And there it lay, on the garden's muddy floor, the curve of its trunk just a hump now; its destroyed beauty produced, even in the faces of its hired executioners, a kind of wonder.

Only Rehan's grandmother, looking, not at the tree, but at the light striking its fleshy stump, was triumphant.

'No rakshasa there, Nani!' Rehan cried out.

She gave him a bitter look. His mother pressed her fingers to the bridge of her nose, seeming to suppress tears.

Rehan glanced over at her and breathed out. 'OK, let's do it.'

'The flat? Really?' she asked, wiping her eyes, surprised at his adult timing.

He looked sadly at her, compacted his lips, and nodded.

*   *   *

Some days later, at the maidan, the effigies awaited their end. Udaya and Rehan, late in arriving, had to watch from the flyover. Here, too, the crowd grew large. Policemen in olive-green uniforms prodded them with canes but when they became too many, they gave up. Rehan, on one rung of the flyover's parapet where a sheet of hoarding, rusted and threatening, had been bent away, felt them press against his legs. He looked urgently down at his mother, already anxious.

'Come down, baba. It's not safe,' she said, feeling his dismay.

'I can't see anything.'

'Nothing has begun yet.'

But it was in snatches that Rehan saw white explosions riddle the first effigy – Ravana's son – and flames climb wildly up the hollow of his body. Then the gaps in the crowd closed. He knew from the roar that rose off the maidan that the burning was over. When he next glimpsed the skeletal frame alight and collapsing, limb by limb, he had to hide his great disappointment. Udaya saw this and felt terrible. It was their first Dussehra and Diwali alone, in the new flat, and everything was significant.

For the second burning she tried carrying him piggy-back but couldn't keep him up. His weight slid down her back, his arms pulled against her neck and hair. At last it was Rehan who said, 'Don't worry, Ma, I can see.' And when the second roar came, he roared louder than the rest.

It was now Ravana's turn. Rehan was preparing to go through the motions again, when from nowhere two powerful arms gripped him by the legs and lifted him out of the crowd. His mother's hand steadied him, and when he looked down, he found himself sitting on the shoulders of a man he had never met before. Ahead, he had a clear view of the demon-king.

His mother's voice, carrying up from the thick crowd below, said: 'Baba, say thank you . . . Amit Uncle.'

'Just Amit is fine,' the man said.

Rehan, though he said a loud thank you, could not make out his face; just the greying hair and spectacles.

Night fell over the maidan. Moths and insects swarmed in the light of naked bulbs and flares. And over the tense and seething mass, bunches of pink balloons and candy-floss bobbed lightly by. Rehan Tabassum's face burned brightly with the fire of the dying Ravana.

2

Dinner for Ten

(1985–2002)

'To awaken to history was to cease to live instinctively. It was
to begin to see oneself and one's group the way the outside
world saw one; and it was to know a kind of rage. India was
now full of this rage. There had been a general awakening.'

India: A Million Mutinies Now, V.S. Naipaul

In those days not even French table wine was available on the open market. Nor was foie gras nor penne. Air conditioners were confined to one room, usually the bedroom. Power cuts were frequent. The majority of foreign cars were second hand. And it was a testament to Amit Sethia's great wealth that on the night of the dinner party he had split-unit air conditioners running freely in all the rooms of his Delhi house, a brand-new Toyota Crown stood in the drive and in the distance the comforting growl of a 40KVA generator was audible. But he was not a magician: for the penne, pâté and wine, he had had to ask a favour of the ambassadors of Italy and France respectively, both countries with which his company had collaborated. They didn't mind; it was part of their diplomatic stock; and besides, they were pleased to be invited to the dinner for the Rajamata.

Amit Sethia didn't chase after royals. 'What royalty?'

he liked to say to his wife. 'An occupying power comes to your country and appoints some local chieftain the king, and two hundred years afterwards, once the power has left, we're still saying, "Hukum this, hukum that." Hukum and fuck 'em, I say. Number one frauds. Not one of these people fought both the Mughal and the British; their very survival is proof of their betrayal. I don't believe in any such royalty.'

'So why did you ask her?' his wife replied, settling a wedge of foie gras onto a creased bed of lettuce, and adding, 'Just like the ones we had at Les Deux Magots in Paris.'

Sethia resented his wife's easy French pronunciation; and, as the person who introduced her to the cafe in question, he did not like her overfamiliarity with the place. '*Café* Deux Magots,' he stressed, then further corrected her: 'besides, we didn't have it there; we had it at Maxim's.' But since this was not the true source of his irritation, he steered the conversation back to where it began: 'You think I invited the old lady because she's the Rajamata of some long forgotten desert kingdom, is it? Not a chance. You and your toady family might feel that way; I certainly don't.'

Sumitra Sethia, though she tolerated a great deal of personal abuse from her husband, could not stand one word said against her family. 'So what then? For charity purposes, you're calling the old lady? "Come one and all to Amit Sethia's langar. You will have pâté, pasta and French wine."' She laughed happily at her joke, and having prepared her first course, she pushed the small ivory plates to one side and began making a dressing. Amit fell into a moody silence. A moment later, he reached past her and picked a canapé of ham and asparagus off a silver tray.

'Amit, don't! Look what you've done? You've ruined the arrangement.' Sumitra readjusted the spacing between the little toasted pieces. 'Bharat Singh!' she yelled. 'Take this tray from here. Or saab will eat them all.' A bearer in white appeared, and smiling mildly, vanished with the tray.

Saab returned to the topic at hand.

'Let me tell you, if they had not honoured me with that Captain of Commerce award, the old lady would never be coming here tonight. But when someone puts forward the cup of friendship, it's not right to spit in it, no matter how bogus the wine might be.'

'Oh-oh, that's it, is it?' his wife replied. But in truth she was won over by this rhetorical effort and her husband could see she was. He smiled pityingly at her reluctance to accept defeat. Then, knowing the admiration she had for him, her willingness always to see things as he saw them, especially in this one regard, he added, 'Yes, and perhaps the old lady gave me something of the glad eye too. You know, she was a famous beauty. Celebrated in Europe and dressed by . . .'

'Yes, yes, by Mainbocher, I know, everyone knows. But not for a long time. Go then. No one's stopping you. You can be her Prince Philip. I give it six months. By then you won't be in the bed, you'll be under it with a bedpan. Then we'll see how sweet the wine tastes.'

Amit Sethia laughed, feeling that this was as good an admission of defeat as any.

'Now you mention it,' he said, walking over to the far end of the kitchen, 'let's see what Jérôme, the Jeroboam, has sent us.' He knew very well what the ambassador had sent; he had told Bharat Singh that morning to put the wine out to settle. 'Saint Julien Ducru-Beaucaillou.' He read the tangerine label while slowly turning the bottle in his hand. 'Very grand,' Sethia muttered, 'very grand. Even the Rajamata is not likely to have drunk anything as good as this.' Then his face soured. 'Bharat Singh! Why have you not put the others out to settle?'

Bharat Singh's face flashed in the greasy pane of the swinging kitchen door. When he saw that it held no answers, frustration tempered only by a love of lecturing arose in Amit Sethia. 'Can you think, Bharat Singh, why I might have asked you to put the wine out to settle?'

Bharat Singh was not in the habit of answering questions directly.

'I thought if we needed more, I would . . .'

'That's not what I asked you,' Amit Sethia growled, 'I *asked* if you knew why I had told you to put the bottle out.'

'Leave it, darling.'

'Sumitra, no. This is important. The boy has to learn.'

'No,' Bharat Singh confessed, feeling perhaps that he was not without allies.

'Good. That's a beginning. I asked you to put the bottle out to settle because with good wine, and especially old wine, there is sediment. It is that that we have to allow to settle at the bottom before we decant the wine. And the reason we do this?'

Bharat Singh now knew he had only to continue with his stance of ignorance.

'So that we can maximize the surface area at which the wine is exposed to oxygen.' So far only 'wine' and 'surface area' had been said in English and already Bharat Singh was lost. 'Isse hum,' Sethia continued, ' "letting the wine breathe" kehlate hein.

'So,' he said, with tenderness for his sudden student,

'if we put one bottle out to settle for the entire day, we must put out every bottle that we intend to drink that day. Samjhe?'

Bharat Singh nodded appreciatively and dived into the pantry from where he emerged seconds later with two more bottles of the wine the ambassador had sent over that morning.

Sethia flashed three fingers at him and smiled conspiratorially.

'Now listen,' his wife said, drawing Sethia's attention away from the pantry door, 'you must give me good warning for dinner. There's pasta so I'll need notice of at least twenty-five minutes to half an hour.'

'Of course, darling. In fact, serve dinner forty minutes after everyone has arrived. And Sumitra . . .'

'Yes,' she said, pushing past the kitchen door.

'Sumitra,' he repeated, in a tone that implied she should look at him.

'What, darling?'

He tapped his teeth with the nail of his index finger; his wet lips glistened broadly in a smile. 'Pasta should be al dente.'

* * *

Amit Sethia would never forget that evening. Years later, when the country had changed beyond recognition, when he had dwarfed all the targets he had set himself, both in real and purchasing power parity terms, when his Crown had been replaced with a Bentley and undisturbed central air conditioning purred through all his houses from Calcutta to Delhi, when he went to the World Economic Forum at Davos and had wine in his 183-bottle Eurocave that put to shame the ambassadors of three Western European countries, when the lawyer-girlfriend he would trade Sumitra for had no cares but the small worry that the marquetry in the plane was not quite right, when there was all this and more, there was still the pain of that dinner. He was unable to rid himself of his one regret: why hadn't he started without the Rajamata?

From the beginning, Sethia had watched his guests arrive, in a strange out-of-drawing-room trance. The slim effeminate Servain, with his youthful face and his buxom wife. Brusetti, the Italian ambassador, with dark greasy hair and a giddy American wife, who spoke continuously about the safety of her children in India. His friend Nair, who disappointed him by wearing a suit and tie. This brought Sethia's soul into sudden hand-in-glove contact with his body. Grabbing hold of the knot of his friend's tie, he gave it a violent tug. 'The cognoscenti don't wear this, my friend. This is worn by those who have to.' Nair gave a confused smile at this unexpected aggression from his friend, but his wife, a large Punjabi woman, brushed Sethia aside, straightened her husband's tie and the couple sailed into the drawing room, leaving Sethia's spirit to drift once more into a stance of watchful distaste. It was eight o'clock.

For the next hour, from this bitter vantage point, Sethia noticed all the failings of his party. Looking down on the room of bright modern art, leather sofas and Lalique objets, his eye fastened on the painful details. Why, for instance, after fifteen minutes, was Brigitte Servain's glass still empty? Why had that idiot Bharat Singh not brought around the canapés? Sethia had to stop himself from running into the kitchen, grabbing armfuls of champagne and canapés and distributing them among his guests like a schoolteacher sending children on a fieldtrip. Eat, eat, drink, drink – there's lots.

The women had taken over the conversation. They were discussing the languages their children would learn to speak simply by growing up in India.

'It's like Switzerland,' Jane Brusetti said in a loud American voice. 'Shane speaks Hindi, English and because the maid is Tamilian, he speaks a smattering of Tamilian too.'

'Tamil,' Nair's wife interceded, and smiled knowingly in Sumitra's direction.

'Sorry?' the ambassador's wife said in confusion.

'Tamil,' Nair's wife repeated, 'the people are Tamilian, the language is Tamil.'

'Oh, sorry, Tamil.'

The Indian women smiled with satisfaction.

What was the need to do that? Sethia silently seethed, bloody provincial woman, forever scoring these small points.

'So yes,' Jane Brusetti continued, 'like Switzerland. Except that instead of French, German, Italian, they're learning, Hindi, English, of course, and *Tamil.*'

'French, German and Italian would have been better,' Brigitte Servain said, causing an icy silence to fall over the room.

These men were not lowly clerks, Sethia thought, they were two high-level diplomats and an important businessman; could they find nothing to talk about except the embassy education of their children? And yet, Sethia himself felt incapable of introducing change. Politics would be too heavy-handed . . . Art! he thought at last.

'Your excellency,' he said, rousing Servain from the smiling placidity into which he had sunk, while also reminding his guests of the company they were in, 'what do you think of Husain?'

The ambassador stared at Sethia in wonderment, as if faced with the diplomatic challenge of his life. Then with a little cough, he began slowly, 'Well, you know, before my posting here in Delhi, I was the deputy ambassador in Tehran.'

'Oh, really!' Nair's wife said aimlessly.

'Yes,' Servain continued, egged on by her enthusiasm, 'and I was always amazed at the passions this man could still awaken in the average Iranian. It was fascinating to see this fifteen-hundred-year history, still so alive in Iran, as if it had happened just yesterday. You should see them on Ashura, beating themselves in his name.'

'Oui, mais c'était affreux,' his wife said.

'Oui, mais, bien sur. But still, Brigitte, amazing. It would be the equivalent in Europe of Italians marching in the streets of Rome because the city was sacked in 400 AD or whatever.'

'No,' Brusetti interjected, 'Jérôme, it's an exaggeration. It would be as if the Spanish were still angry for the Islamic invasions of the eighth century.'

'Yes, fine. But still, hard to imagine.'

Sethia sank into a moody silence, considering with sidelong glances the two M.F. Husain paintings that, hanging in the far end of the room, had inspired his question. It was nine o'clock and Sumitra had disappeared.

She returned a moment later, somewhat frantic. 'When do you want to eat?' she hissed. 'I'm making a slow-roast; it will be spoiled if we wait too long.'

'Can you not see,' Sethia said, coming to the true source of his anxiety, 'that all the guests have not yet arrived?'

'Something must have happened. You should call and find out?'

Over my dead body, Sethia thought to himself. But just then, with the arrival of the ninth guest, a glimmer of hope went through the party. Maggu Mahapatra was a vicious socialite, with ethnic affectations, launched in India and abroad by the Rajamata. Sethia was loath to have him in his house. But dining tables in Delhi, like in other places, were hungry for single men; and, as he went everywhere the Rajamata did, he invariably eased conversation.

He was dressed in a pale shade of brown. His salwar, which tightened around the knees, was of a bright silky material; the long sleeveless coat he wore over his kurta was of a duller, coarser fabric. In his dark slim hand, he carried a broad packet of Dunhills and a lighter. When Sethia leaned in to greet him, he could smell the night air on his clothes, tinged with an oil-based perfume. His twinkling eyes, Sethia felt, had taken in the room and the Rajamata's absence, for before releasing him, he said, as if reading to Sethia's depths, 'She said to say she was on her way. Her nephews drove in from Kusumapur this evening and she's been sitting with them, drinking rum. I love that about her. She switches from Old Monk to DP in a flash.'

The diplomatic circle giggled, as if out of gratitude to Mahapatra for bringing to their dull gathering news of the outside world.

'No rush, no rush,' Sethia said unconvincingly, adding, 'and you, Maggu, you'll have your usual?'

Mahapatra understood the implication. And not to be socially outmanoeuvred by an amateur, he said, 'I'll have a whisky soda. But Amit, what a wonderful house you have! Sumitra, dear, do I see your hand in all of this? I wish I had brought something . . .'

'No, no, what for?' Sumitra said, rushing up.

'Well, one should,' Maggu replied, and stressed: 'at least *the first time* . . .'

'Come, come, Maggu,' Sethia interjected. 'Monsieur . . .'

'Servain. Of course. We met at the opening of my exhibition.'

'How can I forget!' Brigitte Servain said, cutting in. 'Jane, you must meet Maggu Mahapatra, the greatest textile expert in India. He has done the most exquisite things.'

And like this, the diplomatic circle closed around Mahapatra, bringing an atmosphere of great cheer and congeniality to the recently moribund gathering.

But for Sethia there was little joy. The sting of the Rajamata's lateness and Mahapatra's prattle had brought the world suddenly very near; and he saw slights everywhere. In a perverted desire to assert himself and his world, he began a separate conversation with Nair, in loud tones, about capital, equity and leverage. Every now and then, he would interrupt Mahapatra with a wave of his finely manicured hand, flashing emerald and diamond rings of astrological influence. He enjoyed seeing Mahapatra's face fall at the rudeness of the interruption; the champagne gave him a reckless daring; who were these people, after all, to bind him to drawing-room manners? But his interjections were not always successful and were returned with put-downs that only he was able to ignore. His addressing Brigitte Servain, for instance, as 'Hey, darling' was returned with a cold 'Darling to my husband; Brigitte to you.' And his 'Maggu, hey listen, how much liquidity is there in the textile business?' was answered with 'None at all. Unless the roof leaks, which, in my exhibitions, it so often does.'

It was in this hour of pride at his nonconformity that Amit Sethia decided to raise the stakes. Seeing now that it was almost ten o'clock, an idea entered his head. And speaking in a voice that was loud enough for everyone to hear, he told Sumitra from across the room to serve dinner.

'What about the Rajamata?' she rapidly whispered, as she walked by.

'Too bad,' Sethia bravely replied.

Sumitra, who perhaps knew her husband better than he knew himself, cast a questioning look down at him. He pretended not to notice and straightened the rings on his fingers, making them catch the light for his amusement.

If the other guests noticed the exchange, they said nothing.

But no sooner had his wife gone than Amit Sethia felt his resolve break. The eight to ten minutes that the pasta needed were excruciating. They drained him of the light drunkenness that had been the source of his courage. Why was it taking so long? If only they were seated and eating, the wine in the glasses, the candles lit, he wouldn't need any more courage to see the thing through. The deed would be done, the point made.

And so, when Sethia felt Sumitra's hand rest on his shoulders, telling him dinner was served, he wanted to clutch it and kiss it.

'Come,' he said, as if roused from a sleep, his voice growing stronger, 'excellencies, ladies and gentlemen, come, dinner is served.'

Mahapatra took a sip of Scotch and pursed his lips in a gesture of cruel amusement. The guests rose languidly, looking here and there for handbags and shawls left behind. Beyond the glass doors that separated the drawing room from the corridor, another set of glass doors gave onto a dining room where a candlelit table had been laid for ten; on either end of it, two open bottles of red wine stood imposingly on two silver coasters. Just as the party had begun to move through the glass doors, the doorbell rang.

That was when Sethia's courage left him; that was the moment he was never to forget.

The Rajamata stood in his doorway, like a visiting

goddess, framed against the night. She wore a dark-blue silk sari with a silver geometric border, the colours seeming to match the grey of her short, blow-dried hair and the dazzle of a single sapphire on her wrinkled fingers. At the sight of her, the ambassadors folded their hands and lightly bowed their heads; their wives curtsied. A cold smoky wind blew into the corridor as though through a tunnel. Mahapatra rushed ahead and held the Rajamata's frail hand while the diamonds around the sapphire flashed. Sethia's eyes sank to the silver border of the Rajamata's sari, which, with its rising and falling design, seemed to him to describe the fluctuating shape of a lifeline.

Mahapatra was leading her down the row of guests, as though asking her to review a ceremonial guard. She had a word for everyone and when she reached Sumitra, Sethia's last defence against . . . well, himself really, against his weakening will . . . a womanly tenderness entered the Rajamata's manner. She noticed a navratan on Sumitra's neck that Sethia had given her, and fingering it lightly in her creased fingers, she said, in a firm gravelly voice, 'The most beautiful I've ever seen. Your husband?'

Sumitra smiled coyly. The Rajamata beamed; the crow's feet around her eyes scattered. 'Good, beti. I'm glad he's spoiling you; you deserve it.' Sethia knew before she clutched his hand, at once apologizing for her lateness and asking swiftly for a Scotch and soda, that his resolve had shattered. And when guiding the Rajamata into the house, they passed the glass doors of the dining room, through which she spied the table laid for ten, he said, in response to her question – 'Dinner already?' – 'Take your time, Rajamata. There's no hurry; it's a buffet.'

In that instant he hoped that someone present might see the gesture as a gallant one. But turning into the drawing room, Sethia knew from Mahapatra's dancing eyes and the sad contempt in those of his wife that no one had forgotten his bluster of a few moments before.

At first, Sethia had no regrets. But when the guests had resumed their places in the drawing room and cheer returned to the party, which Mahapatra was now savagely dominating, Sethia felt a stab of pain. From the corner of his eye, past two sets of glass doors, he saw Bharat Singh snuff out the candles on the virgin dining table; a rapid stream of smoke climbed into the spotlit emptiness of the room. More lights came on and one by one the dinner arrangement was undone, cutlery reassembled and re-laid. A tall stack of plates, interleaved with napkins, appeared at one corner of the dining table. Sethia could see rapid figures moving across the greasy pane of tube light in the kitchen door. He imagined his wife trying to salvage the pasta; or simply binning it, and wondering how she would present her delicate starter of lettuce and pâté, so clearly intended for a small single plate, in the form of a buffet.

When the first plates appeared on napkined laps in his drawing room, Sethia saw in the lettuce drooped sadly over the pâté, in the heap of soggy orange pasta around which the pink juices of the meat ran freely, the full calamity of what had befallen his dinner party. His wine, which was to have been decanted, stood precariously, like some university plonk, on a stack of coffee-table books.

Mahapatra was entertaining the room, and especially the Rajamata, with a story of Sita Baroda, the last wife of the Maharaja of Baroda, who after Independence, had made off with the Baroda jewels.

'When they realized they were gone, she was already in Ceylon. She was at a state dinner when a message came from India to the Governor General of Ceylon, instructing him to "Arrest that woman." The Governor General replied, "I can hardly arrest her; she's on my right."'

The diplomatic women shrieked with laughter. Brigitte Servain said, 'No, it's too good.'

The Rajamata smiled with pleasure, then said, 'Maggu, tell the story of Honey Hohenlohe and Sita Baroda.'

'From the Club Marbella?' Maggu asked.

The Rajamata nodded and sipped her whisky.

'Well, Honey Hohenlohe, as you know,' Maggu began, '*owned* the Club Marbella. And so one night Sita Baroda was there and was banging on about Baroda and titles, and how she was HRH and Honey was only HSH, Her Serene Highness, and so finally she says, "And in Baroda, I receive a twenty-one gun salute," at which point, Honey, a big blonde Texan, who couldn't give a fuck, says, "I bet you do, darling. Right up your big black ass."'

As laughter filled his drawing room Sethia felt his hatred reach a pinnacle and crystallize. Look at these mediocrities, he thought, eating my wine and drinking my food, while holding me in contempt. Who are these people with their false manners, making me feel small in my own house? These third-rate princes, who were meant to defend us from foreign occupation, and who each became a worse toady than the other. Here, their descendants sit now, with the ambassadors of the same powers that ennobled them and turned them into puppets, regaling them with banal tales of European drawing rooms. While I, who have worked twice as hard and given back twice as much, am like a sort of businessman fool footing the bill.

But what could he do? His protest was gone, his fight forfeited. And to complete the last of what had been an evening of incomplete gestures, he rose, and without a word to anyone, went upstairs and got into bed.

His last memory was a late-night image of his wife in blouse and petticoat, taking off her jewellery before a dimly lit dressing table.

'I hope I was not too rude . . .' he said in sleep and partial hope.

'Don't worry,' she replied archly, putting the last of her gold bangles in a shallow silver tray, 'they didn't even notice.'

* * *

The years crawled and then raced. A new energy seeped into every corner of life in India. The memory of that time of shortages faded. And with that change, as purchasing power parities turned to real terms, men like Sethia grew into giants overnight. Business ceased to be one of many stories; it became the only story. And the people who visited India in those new decades did not seek out the princes as they once had; they sought out men like Sethia.

But Sethia never forgot. He never forgave himself that

on that night, now lost in the darkest folds of the 1980s, when no one had known that the country was on the eve of change, he had not had the courage to be the man he intended to be. And he was not above settling scores. In fact his antipathy for the princes had surpassed the Rajamata's person, now old and frail, and had extended to all the descendants of all those families to whom gun salutes of any number, ranging from one to twenty-one, had ever been offered.

Just before the close of the decade, he had tried to avenge himself with the Maharaja of Gwalior.

The Maharaja had entered politics and wanted to meet Sethia as part of the regular fund-raising activities politicians conduct at election time. Sethia readily agreed to see him. They sat in the study of his old Lutyens Delhi house. Across from them, on the desk, were crested silver frames containing pictures of the Maharaja's family with other princes and British dignitaries as well as a large collection of coloured stone lingas.

Sethia, after several minutes of stilted conversation, over the course of which he agreed to give the Maharaja the ten lakhs he wanted for his campaign, looked somewhat aimlessly over at the desk and muttered, 'The junk the princes collected!'

The Maharaja was not sure he had heard right.

'I'm sorry?'

'I said,' Sethia repeated, 'the junk you princes collected.'

At this the young Maharaja laughed uproariously. 'You couldn't be more right,' he said, 'when I go through some of my father's and grandfather's things, I'm filled with shame. I think of the incredible bronzes and stone sculpture that it was possible for them to have made collections of. And what do we have instead? Porcelain seals. Paperweights. Models of European landmarks. Nudes by forgotten artists. What can I say? Except that I think, with colonization, we forgot our points of reference.'

Sethia sank into a dissatisfied silence. This was not the reaction he had hoped for. He felt like a man forced to swallow a ball of phlegm he had been ready to spit out. Then, tucking in the crimped and fan-shaped end of his lungi between his legs, he said to the Maharaja, 'How come you have chosen to meet me in your bed clothes?'

The prince looked puzzled. He gazed down at his kurta pajama, and with great hesitation, fearful he was compromising his ten lakhs, said at last: 'I'm not sure I know what you mean.'

'Ah!' Sethia said, and continuing with musical fluency, added, 'I was told by my elders that pajamas were to be worn between the bathroom and the bedroom, and never, if it could be helped, in the corridor.'

The Maharaja's confusion grew; he felt perhaps that a joke had been made, but he was not sure. He smiled uneasily; Sethia's expression remained stern and expectant.

'One has to compromise,' the Maharaja said at last, in as mollifying a tone as he could manage.

Sethia's face turned to disgust, as though he had lost respect for his adversary. He rose to leave. 'You'll have your money, Gwalior. You should have asked for more while you had the chance.'

With this, he was gone.

*   *   *

The nineties, which with the coming of Coca-Cola, Ruffles potato crisps and MTV brought more hope than the high principles of the years before had ever done, made a new man of Amit Sethia. In this spring of liberalization, when most men his age were consolidating their gains, the possibilities that opened up returned him to the full bloom and vitality of his youth. He bought new cars, Brioni suits, he travelled abroad every month, he switched his drink from Black Label to Dom Pérignon, he fell in love again. He thought of the years that lay on the other side of the change as wasted years; he summed up Sumitra in his heart as 'pre-liberalization', dooming her to the deadest of dead pasts. And though she remained in his home for many years, he had begun to see other women, particularly a young lawyer. But, at dinner on her barsati only a few weeks after they met, Amit Sethia was reminded that the past was not yet behind him.

It was May. They ate outside on one of the last nights when it was possible to do so. Udaya had lit the terrace with glass fanooses; they had, between the two of them, drunk the champagne Amit had brought as well as most of a bottle of what Pappu, the bootlegger, his cellars now brimming with new varieties, described as 'polee fussee'.

'Use mine,' Udaya had said, when Amit asked for the bathroom. 'Rehan is sleeping in the other room.'

He had gone in good spirits, but returned with a contemptuous smile.

'So,' he said, 'I see that you're one of those.'

'One of whom?' Udaya asked in confusion.

'One of those who run behind every third-rate little shit of a prince.'

'Excuse me,' Udaya said, hardly able to gauge his meaning past the violence of his language. Seeing her face fall, Amit controlled himself, and began speaking in more measured tones. 'I see you've put up a picture of Maggu Mahapatra and that gandu prince, what's his name, Tuttu . . .'

'Retaspur,' Udaya asserted firmly, 'both old friends. And one now dead, so please go easy on him.'

'Good, good that he's dead. What else do you expect when you drink all day, and get it in the ass from truck drivers and servants at night. Yellow fingers, the lot of them, all yellow fingers.'

'What's wrong with you, Amit?' Udaya said, flaring up. 'I said that he was a friend and he's dead. What is this venom?'

'Venom!' Amit exploded. 'Calling me venomous? And praising those shits, those third-rate good-for-nothings. Friends! They're nobody's friends; they just collect courtiers. That's what you were: a courtier, a little hanger-on. And me, I suppose I'm nothing to you. I don't see my picture anywhere in your house.'

'Is mine in yours?' Udaya asked, frigid with anger, smiling slightly.

Amit Sethia lost all composure. His eyes bulged, his lips ran dry, and the voice that broke from his throat was as loud and coarse a thing as Udaya had ever heard. 'You're just a little climber! Why don't you go and suck Maggu Mahapatra . . .'

In all fairness to Amit Sethia, he had not meant for the words to come out that way. His idiomatic English was not entirely under his control, and he had, in all probability, meant something more along the lines of 'suck up to' rather than what he actually said. But, under the circumstances, it was impossible for Udaya to say anything other than what she did say, in an icy threatening whisper: 'Get out!'

Amit Sethia rose and swept his spectacles off the table, glancing for a moment at what must have seemed like an apparition in the doorway of the barsati. When he had gone, Rehan, in his white night suit, approached his mother cautiously. 'Who was that man, Ma,' Rehan asked with trepidation, 'was he the same one who came that day on Dussehra? Who is he?'

For a moment she didn't answer. Then clutching the little hand that rested on her shoulder, she swung around, and with eyes glittering in the candlelight, said, 'A good man, baba. A good man. Just one who is a little angry.'

The next day, before Udaya and Rehan woke, the early morning joggers and walkers of Golf Links were treated to the spectacle of a dozen bouquets, half a spring almost, and at least two entire flower shops – and not just roses, but orchids and lilies in May – encircling the watchman's bunk at number 187.

And then, one cold winter day, almost in our present time, when Sethia's hair had turned white, and he had grown it to shoulder length, during a period of his life that Udaya described as 'Menoporsche', the opportunity to settle his ancient score arose.

That year, the World Economic Forum, due to the terrorist attacks in America, was being held in New York. Sethia was staying at the Four Seasons on 57th Street. After a breakfast session with Musharraf, he returned to his room, turned on the television and picked up the phone to call Udaya. When the long, mournful ringing gave way to her voice, he put the television on mute. The images flashed silently before him as Udaya's energetic chatter filled the space that the television's noise had left. She wanted to know what the weather was like; how was Musharraf? Did he seem serious about peace with India? Had Amit bought the three bottles of Jo Malone's Tuberose that she had asked for? Amit half-listened while resting his gaze on the television. Udaya was trying to convince him to visit the college Rehan was due to attend that summer.

'How can I, darling? It's in Massachusetts.'

'So?'

'What do you mean "so"? I'm in New York. It's like asking someone to see a college in Amritsar on a trip to Delhi.'

'You know, Amit, unless he feels you care . . .'

'Tch, Udaya! I care, but I'm not going a hundred and fifty miles to see his college. Besides, they're all the same, these liberal artsy places. If he really wants to do arts and literature, he may as well do it in India. I don't see why I should pay thirty thousand dollars a year for him to read novels in America.'

'Suit yourself, but then don't complain to me that . . .'

'Wait, wait, Shhh, Udaya, one second.'

'What is it?'

But there was no reply. The images now appearing on the television held Sethia's attention so completely that it was a second before he realized the sound was off.

'Amit?'

'I'll call you back,' he said in a furtive whisper and absent-mindedly hung up. Then turning on the sound to the special hour-long remembrance, he watched and listened in horror. Under a black and white oval photograph of a thirties beauty, it said 'The Rajamata of Kusumapur, 1919–2002'.

The sky outside was grey; the wind thumped against his window; there was a hint of snow. The goose-down bed and the darkness of the room seemed to muffle him. On the television, images of the Rajamata, as in a slideshow, went moodily in and out of focus. They showed her at Ascot. In chiffon and pearls, awarding a polo trophy. In white at the pyre of her dead husband. With Prince Philip and the Queen. With Jackie Kennedy. Released from Tihar Jail after the Emergency. Sethia watched, as if waiting for an image from that fateful night to appear. But of course it never came. The Rajamata was going, free of her sins, into that edited heaven of coffee-table books and one-hour specials.

Sethia should have gone back to the forum; there were other sessions to attend; but he found he didn't have the will. He decided, in the hope of taking his mind off his shock at the Rajamata's death, to step out to buy Udaya's perfume. Perhaps he would buy Rehan something too; Udaya would notice if he didn't.

He dressed lightly despite the cold, and passing the full-length mirror on the way out was momentarily detained by his reflection. He was old. His body had shrunk, his shoulders had turned in at the corners and a dark length of flesh, stubbled white, hung lower from his chin than he would have thought possible. But he also recognized an old fire in his face, and no sooner had he squared eyes with it than it consumed all trace of weakness. No, it was death to let anything go; he would keep it all very near to him, 'the grief and the glory'.

Downstairs, the lobby swarmed with Indians. Sethia swelled with pride at the thought that he was a living record of the time when his countrymen had been pygmies abroad, restricted to twenty dollars a day. And now, here they were, thinking nothing of paying five hundred a night for a room. He remembered when even he had had to eat at fast-food restaurants and delis; but now, at any moment, the pretty blonde concierge would walk over to tell him that his reservation that night at Jean Georges was confirmed. And it was as he scanned the lobby for her that he caught sight of a familiar figure gliding across its marble floor.

Though the hair now was grey and there was an ashen cast over his once glowing skin, he was unmistakable in his quilted kaftan and still held a broad packet of Dunhills in his hands. The distress in his face was visible even at a distance.

'Maggu!' Sethia said, hurrying up to him with a broad smile.

Mahapatra stopped and swivelled around. A glazed look of disappointment entered his eyes.

'Hello, Amit,' he said.

'Don't tell me! The great Indian socialist at the WEF?'

'No,' Mahapatra replied coldly, 'I have a textile exhibition at the Met.'

'I'm sorry for your loss,' Amit said, now smiling more broadly than ever, 'I thought you would have been by her side at the last.'

'I was, till just the other day. But then she was better and said I should go. She went fast, and in peace.'

'And you're not Master of Ceremonies at the funeral?'

'I'm flying tomorrow,' Maggu said wearily, 'with Chitra.'

'Chitra?'

'The Rajamata's great-niece.'

'She lives here, in New York?' Sethia asked with fresh interest.

'Yes,' Maggu replied, 'in this hotel in fact.'

An incredulous expression crossed Sethia's face. He was about to say something when Mahapatra pre-empted him.

'She's a student of hotel management, here as a

trainee. They're turning the Kusumapur Palace into a hotel.'

'Ah!' Sethia said with satisfaction. 'I thought so. Otherwise, where could those broken-down princes afford to stay here? That's all they can do now, I suppose. Hawk their last few possessions, turn their palaces into hotels and use their names while they still can.'

'Yes, OK. Well, nice to see you, Amit. Some other time. Give my love to Udaya.'

Before he could say anything else Maggu was gone, leaving Sethia with a new and deeper malaise.

Sethia was about to step out of the hotel but instead he let the revolving doors take him back into the lobby. He headed in long strides for the concierge's desk. His blonde favourite was not there; in her place was a tall black man, who managed to greet Sethia while artfully bringing a phone conversation to an end.

'Mr Sethia,' he said, 'how can I help you?'

'I'm looking,' Sethia began, 'for an employee of yours, who happens to be the niece of a very dear friend of mine from India.'

The concierge stared in wonder at this wide range of connections operating in the place where he worked.

'From India? Wow! What is her name?'

Sethia hesitated and then said, 'I'm not sure of the department, but her name would be Chitrangada Singh of Kusumapur.'

The concierge baulked, then laughed. 'You're going to have to spell that.'

Sethia had just begun to do so when the concierge said, 'Wait, wait, I know her. Chitra from New Delhi. I know her. She works in the spa.'

'In the spa?' Sethia said, unable to contain his delight. 'What does she do there?'

The concierge shrugged his shoulders. 'I'm not sure, but they're usually made to do everything from manning the gym floor to handling the reservations desk, manicures, massage, I don't know,' he said, and laughing, added, 'feed the epidermis-nibbling fish.'

But Sethia was not listening. A plan took shape in his mind.

'Darius,' he said, conspicuously reading the concierge's name pin, 'will you do me a favour? Will you send her a message saying that a friend of her family is staying at the hotel and would like to take her out for a drink this evening? If she's free, she should meet me at seven in the bar.'

Darius was nodding his head, hastily scribbling down the information. Sethia thanked him and hurried up to his room.

* * *

He waited that night in the bar, drinking Laurent-Perrier rosé alone. 'So she hasn't come,' he said to himself, when he saw the clock strike eight, 'works in a spa, massaging strange men, but thinks she is too good to meet Amit Sethia. Chal, we'll see about that.' Though a drunken aggression grew in him, he was not angry. He was pleased she had not come; the second part of his plan depended on her not coming; in fact, he was not sure what he would have done had she actually shown up.

A little before nine he went upstairs and changed into a large Four Seasons robe, with a nap as soft as velvet, and a matching pair of towelling slippers. He liked to walk though the hotel's carpeted corridors dressed like this; it made him feel he was above caring for the proprieties the hotel inspired in others.

In the spa, the air was suffused with the faint smell of eucalyptus oil. An atmosphere part clinic, part afterlife pervaded the place. There were bamboo screens and narrow channels of water lined with floating candles.

Attendants in white hurried about him, speaking in whispered tones. He allowed himself to be led into a dark room, stopping only to ask if his choice of masseuse had been honoured. But he didn't have to wait long for an answer.

In the room itself, where soft music played, he saw a girl in uniform, who for all her diffidence and servile manners, had a Kusumapur face. He knew those features immediately: the thick black hair, the large limpid eyes, the thin stern lips. She stood in the ghostly light emanating from a steaming fountain full of white pebbles. And for a moment, even Amit Sethia was shocked by the irreverence of it all. It was always the West, he thought; the West that had turned these small local rajas into exotic royalty; and the West now that offered them up as masseuses and spa attendants. What are they really? And what are we in relation to them? Who was to know?

He closed the door behind him and pushed off his robe in one swift movement. He thought he saw the trainee-princess steel her expression at the sight of this old naked man from India. Then climbing onto the massage bed, he let his face sink into its hollow. The darkness behind him seemed to expand, and a moment later, drops of warm scented oil fell lightly on his legs and feet. Soon he felt the first brush of those little hands against his body. And in the large granite bowl below him, Amit Sethia saw, from the light of a floating candle, its thin aluminium base bounded in with pink orchids, the smiling face of a man at peace. His revenge was at last secreting its satisfactions.

But what revenge could be exacted privately? To be complete, it had to be acknowledged. And practising what he would say, he mouthed the words into the cavity below him, too soft for her to hear: 'I'm sorry for your loss.' Yes, that would do it. Those little royal hands would stop their work and all that needed to be said would be said. But even with victory so near, Sethia found himself strangely incapable of saying the words aloud. Was it weakness, the same lack of courage as that night many years ago? He didn't think so. But then what was it? What was preventing him from taking something that was so justly his? He wondered if the silence and darkness of the room had subdued him. If, perhaps, he was to get a conversation going, he would feel more emboldened.

His questions came innocently at first. How long had she been here? Eighteen months. Where in India did she come from? A small central state. Which borough of New York did she live in? Brooklyn, but she was hoping to move to Manhattan soon. She answered in a calm steady voice, like any young person doing work experience in a big city. But with the easy flow of conversation, Sethia found he was, if anything, further away from saying the words that would seal his revenge.

The minutes passed and he could tell from her progression over his body that time was running out. He thought perhaps it was a logistical problem. After all, how could he say anything when his face was buried in this hole? That was it. He would wait for them to be face to face, then he would see her haughty expression crumble. Sethia began to prepare for the moment she would ask him to turn over, and then he would say, 'You're certainly a long way from Kusumapur!' How funny and satisfying that would be. Yes, that was it; he was just allowing the anticipation to build until he was face to face with her.

And finally, the moment came. He heard her voice softly ask him to turn over. But as soon as he had, even before he had, while the pressure points of his hard cracked heels were being pressed, he was struck by a terrible feeling of pity. His heart went out to this young girl working the night her great-aunt had died. The small flat in Brooklyn. The long flight back to India. The decay of that life, the banality of this one. And suddenly he was filled with a feeling of protective pride for this little Maratha princess. She was not someone so far removed from him, he thought with sudden pain; she was, as he had once been, just one more person India had let down.

When Chitra and Sethia were finally face to face, she looked down on a man who wore an expression wretched with grief, a man who had exacted more revenge than he could handle, and wanted no more massage. He rose fast and apologetically, reaching in the darkness for his robe. 'It was very good. Fine, yes, fine.' It was just that he was old and got tired easily these days. 'I hope you understand. Please. And good luck with everything. Good luck in India.'

Oh, what had he said! He hoped she had not heard. He made quickly for the door, but his feet were oily and the floor slippery. He couldn't find his slippers in the dark. He had managed to pick his way to the door, when he heard her say from the blackness behind him: 'I'm sorry I wasn't able to come this evening. It's just that I do this work . . . and it can be embarrassing to meet people from India who know my family.'

The door was open. A crack of light cleaved the massage room in half. They stood for a moment that way as long shadows and little people. With voice hoarse and eyes turning to glass, Sethia said, 'We are not embarrassed, beti. We are never embarrassed. Life is too short. God bless.'

And saying this, he hurried away into the comfortless tranquillity of soft music and aromatic oils.

3

Notes from a Burglary

(2005)

'It is the responsibility of free men to trust and to celebrate what is constant – birth, struggle, and death are constant, and so is love, though we may not always think so – and to apprehend the nature of change, to be able and willing to change. I speak of change not on the surface but in the depths – change in the sense of renewal. But renewal becomes impossible if one supposes things to be constant that are not – safety, for example, or money, or power.'

The Fire Next Time, James Baldwin

On a day in July, when Delhi's skies whitened, and I was in my last year of college in America, a period of extended isolation came abruptly to an end. Jasbir Singh Jat (ASI), the first to arrive on the scene, trailed the house's high green walls, pointing to places where a breach might have occurred.

'Crossing could have happened here, Rehan saab,' he said, 'and, here.' He grabbed hold of the rusted supports that propped up rolls of razor-wire on the boundary wall, and defying the whiteness of his stubble, swung himself easily onto one corner. There, standing among cement dust and embedded shards of glass, he said, 'And, here, too, a crossing could have been made.'

His uniform was of a coarse greenish-brown material with a single star on the epaulettes. He had a hard prominent jaw and a changeable manner, now grim, now crude and mocking. It was as if, by the sheer robustness of his personality, whether playful or violent, he would ferret out the thief.

But he wanted first to let me know the challenges of his job. He made a charge through the house sizing up the men he passed; he occasionally fell into a sofa, and from that sprawling posture, screwing up his eyes like a comic book detective, took in the room. When passing my bedroom, I asked him how a fifty kilogram safe could have gone missing from the adjoining room without my hearing a sound. 'The thieves, Rehan saab,' Jat replied, 'are very clever; they sometimes pump ammonia into the room. You would have slept the sleep of the dead.'

We sat down at last in the foyer to wait for the forensics team. The security from the night before, Group Four men, one of Delhi's best security agencies, stood around. Jat asked them where they were from. They were heavyset men with local Haryana accents like Jat's. And when he recognized the village from which they came, his suspicions lifted. 'They're family men,' he said to me, 'they wouldn't have done it.'

But they were all family men. And the man on whom the security had first laid their suspicion was not just any family man, he was our family man, of almost eight years. At that stage we had known only of the two missing laptops. And because the security had seen him leave, according to their register, at 9.12 the night before, with a large bag slung over his shoulder, he became our first suspect.

'Oh God, I hope it's not Sati,' my mother had said on the phone, 'it would be such a shame. I think it must be Kalyan. He's forever in trouble with money, taking loans here and there. I think he realized after I told him his family couldn't stay that he was in danger of losing his job. He has to go.' She paused and said, 'Have you checked to see if anything else is missing, the silver, the safe . . .'

That was when Kalyan had entered the room, having less than an hour before discovered the missing laptops.

The tone of the morning had been set by a strange text message from an American friend in Spain. It read: 'Hope you're safely back in India now. I think of you often and I hope that all is well where you are. Beware of complacency, my friend, and work hard. Did you get the recipe for gazpacho?'

Zack. A friend from college studying abroad. I had been with him in Seville only weeks before, on my way back to India for the summer. It would have been late at night in Spain; I imagined he would have drunk too much, even though the message was not uncharacteristic. A few minutes later Kalyan had come in with the tea tray and the two almonds, two walnuts and dozen raisins a nutritionist had advised I eat first thing in the morning. I drank the tea in bed, then went in for a shower. It was not yet six when I rang Kalyan to ask him for a cup of coffee downstairs in my study.

The study was new. Till just the other day it had been the Sethia wine cellar. But now for the past month or so, besides two glass-fronted wine refrigerators, the basement room contained a coffee table, two rattan chairs and a Gustavian writing desk with blue painted legs. On its polished surface lay a brass ashtray, a silver Mac and a desk lamp with a green glass shade.

The new study was a bad room to work in. The buzz from the wine fridges and voltage stabilizers was maddening. The room also had a problem with damp. One entire wall of fresh orange paint had blistered. The surface swelled and cracked. My eye, trailing the contours of the sodden patches, was tempted to think of them as continents on a three-dimensional map. I was fighting the temptation to crush Asia in my fingers when Kalyan appeared in the doorway with a coffee mug.

He put it down on the desk and was turning to leave, when he stopped, and making matter-of-fact the tremor in his voice, said, 'You know, baba, those two laptops that lie upstairs on madam's desk . . .'

'Yes,' I replied, reluctantly turning my mind to them.

'Do you have them downstairs with you?'

A stupid question. They were old and slow and out of use. They never moved from their place on my mother's desk. What's more, I could tell that Kalyan recognized the stupidity of the question, because he spoke now like a servant, playing up his stupidity. And he didn't need to; he was stupid anyway. That he thought I might be fooled by this show of innocence was an even greater stupidity. But servants were often like this: they played with depths, leaving you to wonder whether they might still have greater depths.

'No, Kalyan. Why would they be?'

'Because they're not upstairs any more.'

Save for his large eyes, seemingly kohled and liquid, growing wide with alarm, his face shrank. His small mouth twitched, its expressiveness concealed by a limp black moustache.

'What do you mean not there?' I said, getting up from the desk.

We climbed the short flight of stairs leading from the basement to my mother's study. Kalyan's voice came like an echo from the stairwell, mumbling about how he had come into the study, seen they were not there, thought perhaps I had taken them . . .

They were gone. Their absence left a noticeable gap on the long table. Their chargers were gone too, but the rest of the room was undisturbed.

'Call the security!' I said in a loud voice to Kalyan. And as he went off, I added threateningly, 'Kalyan, this is no small matter. They better be found.'

'Yes, yes,' he said, untying the strings of his black and white apron and rushing off.

The house was called Steeple Hall. It was part of Farmhouse Delhi, a new and privileged urban isolation, initiated some three decades before on the margins of the city. But it was a cautious sanctioning and the men in charge dithered over the luxuries of this new life. They expressed their fears, and socialist resentments, by sometimes placing limits on the square footage of the farmhouses, confining them on occasion to the size of an apartment in town. Then successive dispensations, feeling perhaps that it was absurd to expect anyone to leave Delhi only to live in a house no bigger than a flat, would stretch that limit. It was in this happy period that the original Steeple Hall, allowed six thousand feet, had been built. But by the time Amit Sethia had bought it for my mother, the limit had shrunk again to two thousand. And out of fear that in this season of reeled-in freedoms, my mother could end up with a smaller house than the one she wished to demolish, she was advised to keep the walls of the original structure standing; they would defend their plinth. Inside, of course, she could do what she liked.

The restriction made it impossible for my mother to have the house she wanted. It was to have been an old Delhi house with courtyards, verandas and balconies, a kind of celebration of space following the barsati years; there was to have been a generous use of red sandstone; I think my mother would have wanted a high-pointed arch somewhere, a garden pavilion or two. And though, oddly enough, in the house she ended up with these latter structures were present, as in fact – save for the courtyard – was the rest, the house was not an old Delhi house.

Despite tearing off half a dozen green cement steeples from the original structure, reshaping and reordering rooms, punching in windows where there had been none, there was nothing my mother could do to ennoble the meanness of the house's proportions. Its ceilings were low – made lower still by a false ceiling, installed to hold flat-panelled air conditioners with four vents – and as a result the rooms though well sized forever felt poky. An abrupt and dreary staircase of many short flights and brushed steel banisters hung through the house. There were concealed fluorescent lights and, on the insistence of the architect, sealed glass windows. *This*, in a city where for six months of the year air conditioners were not needed! My mother's decorator brother-in-law, who in memory of the deposed steeples had suggested the name, Steeple Hall, described it now as a cross between a mosque and an IT centre.

The latter part of that description was aimed at the house's drab rectangularity, the former at a giant stand-alone Islamic arch in pink Dholpur stone. It had been pinned, with the help of steel beams, to one side of the building. And, as with the balconies and verandas, it had been part of an imagined cohesiveness. But projecting now, off one face of the building, its base sinking into the side of a grassy hill, the Dholpur stone pale and pinkish in the floodlights, it seemed to jeer at my mother's original intention. It was like the balconies, which had been slung onto the building with the help of iron girders, now each covered in rust, their black paint flaking. Or the verandas, which had pushed back rooms already cheated of their proportions.

But Steeple Hall, for all its flaws, possessed that rarest of rare attributes. With its jagged skyline of triangles where there had been steeples, its giant Islamic arch of the wrong stone, its many blue and white awnings like those seen by a swimming pool and its Hindu figurines — Amit Sethia's influence — dotting the lawn, each with a floodlight of its own, it was by any assessment a house that had gone wrong enough to be right. It had natural lunacy. And once the miniatures and big Persian carpets went in, along with the deep sofas, goose-down pillows and White Company sheets — this was the fourth house my mother had decorated and she did it with the ease of the British laying down a town — it also had comfort.

To this my stepfather, ever a man of the times, added his own technological element: wireless Internet, a modern gym, flat screens and DVD players, Tata Sky and dark-brown plug points capable of taking the plugs of the world. And so, despite having shown the greatest reluctance to do so, Steeple Hall came together as a house, standing as a monument to the cultural confusions that had taken root in India during the early part of the twenty-first century.

It was a place I had begun to come to nearly every weekend from Amit Sethia's company house in town. I was at the end of my third year in college in Massachusetts and in the middle of what I imagined was a significant private transformation. It had its origins in my friendship with Zack, which had begun in our first year. Zack was a slim, handsome mulatto from the Midwest, who had spoken early on to me of his 'protestant work ethic'. And already in those first weeks, when everybody was drinking beer from plastic cups and enjoying the good weather, I would see him putting his words into action.

Every day he went directly from his classes to the sunless C-section of the Robert Frost Library. He remained there, in that gloomy basement till four-thirty, surfacing only for a hurried cigarette. Dressed in stained khakis and a flimsy blue shirt, under which a white vest was visible, he could be seen pacing the library's granite steps, tensely studying the reference cards he had filled, in an abrupt jagged hand, with notes from his afternoon's reading. If anyone approached him, he would look at the person for a moment or so with the terrifying aspect of the Nietzschean solitary, wild-faced and fresh out of the cave. Then this expression would give way to an unnatural smiling manner that would send the intruder faster on his way than the grimmer visage.

At four-thirty he would break for dinner, which meant a short trip to the dining hall where he packed himself two sandwiches in brown paper napkins. Then he would return to the library for the rest of the evening. At close to nine, if I was lucky, I would be summoned for a drink. This occasion, though it had the outward appearance of a festivity, was no less utilitarian. It was a ninety-minute session in which Zack smoked Black & Mild cigars while hastily drinking from a gallon bottle of Carlo Rossi's red wine, spilling it here and there, further staining his khakis. Over the course of these ninety minutes, after which I would be ushered out of his room, he would speak, drink and smoke with the force of a man wishing to relax his mind for sleep. And as it softened, the day's reading poured out of him, bringing a variety of writers and musicians my way: Du Bois, Ellison, James Baldwin; Nina Simone and Coltrane; Baudelaire and Arthur Rimbaud.

Zack was absorbed with aesthetic questions, that though outwardly technical, were, in fact, about the aim of art. Questions of narrative, what you kept, what you left out; the function of economy; the importance of discovering one's material, of looking inward to see which of the stories we contained were important and worth telling. At the beginning of our acquaintance, I had treated Zack's concern with these questions as one of the many pretentious conversations I had routinely had in college. Part of the reason for this was that I myself had never thought to question the purpose of my education.

I had come blindly to college in America from India because it was the thing to do. It was an extension of other forms of entitlement, like summer holidays in the

West, or the buying of a nice car. I don't think I could have answered the question of why I was going to college; not, at least, on my own terms; in my heart, I would have known it was to impress those around me. It was like Tolstoy's youthful fascination with the idea of being *comme il faut.* And this desire to impress others would have extended to what I hoped to learn at the college as well: fashionable French and Russian writers, whose names would serve me well at cocktail parties. The college, too, with its broad surveys of literature and performing professors, was complicit in the acquisition of this kind of learning.

But Zack was different. And, in our third year, still wishing to discover what gifts lay within him, what his responsibility to his talent was, he quit all his reading and writing classes to become a painter. Listening to him one night talk of 'negative space' in his paintings, which he described as the equivalent of 'what is left unsaid' in a story, I began to feel that Zack was crossing the line between education that was ornamental, there to impress others, and education that was real.

Inspiring though his self-improvement was, it gave me a feeling of shame at my own wasted years, at the books read fast and for no other reason than to say I had read them. I wanted to go back and to read again.

I had, by then, acquired the aspiration to be a writer, but feared very much that it was no more profound than that initial desire to go to college in America. I wanted now to look again at its motivations and see if there was really anything there. And that was why I came to Steeple Hall, to read and be alone.

Through this entire period of self-examination, with all its vanities, I had not once thought seriously about my childhood and adolescence in India. All that had remained remote, all still very quiet, still in its preservative, my assumptions and entitlements safely in place. And this was strange, for though I was returning to India for the summer to read and think about my writing ambition, I had not considered it important to think hard about India, which had made me, and which was experiencing significant change of her own. No; I was wilfully keeping her at bay, wilfully taking her for granted. And Steeple Hall, with its new study, gym, large lawns, ponds and pavilions, was – or so, I thought – the ideal place to do so.

In the first few days of my arrival, I set myself an iron-cast routine of reading and exercise. I ate little, drank little and worked hard. I felt at the end of the day mentally and physically fatigued, but full of piety, as if nothing was more important than this private enrichment. But it had not been in place two weeks, my new routine, when Kalyan broke into it with news of the missing laptops.

He returned some moments later with the security guards wearing uniforms in two shades of blue. They were burly men with thick stubble and lidded eyes. They filled the little landing with their size and smell, sweat and sleep mingled together. And there was something unresponsive about them. They knew nothing; they had seen nothing; they heard nothing. Sati, leaving the property the night before with large bags, was the only information they had. I warned them that if the laptops were not found they would all lose their jobs. They nodded gravely but seemed unperturbed. I sent them to search the premises and servants' quarters. Then I turned to Kalyan and fixed my gaze on him. He returned my stare with a look of vacancy and exaggerated innocence.

'Go and search the house,' I barked, 'and see if anything else is missing.'

Next I called Sati. The Telegu film song he had set as his caller ringtone, with its mournful rising and falling rhythms, played through many cycles. My mind was quick to interpret the delay as proof of guilt. One missed call in changed circumstances, and that too, at 6.30 a.m. on a man's day off, was enough to erase a decade of trust.

But the call was not missed. Sati answered just before

it rung off. And this raised other suspicions: Why was he awake at this hour? I had given him the day off. Why this readiness to answer the phone?

He listened gloomily to my account of what had happened. I mentioned his unchecked bag but he made no reply, saying simply that he was on his way. Had he considered it beneath him to defend himself? I went back into the study and called my mother.

That was when, timed with Kalyan re-entering the room, she said, '. . . Have you checked to see if anything else is missing, the silver, the safe . . . ?'

I was about to ask Kalyan about the safe, when using an English word, he pre-empted me: 'Baba, that box of madam's that she keeps in her cupboard, has she, by any chance, taken it with her?'

'You mean the safe, Kalyan?' I said, offering the Hindi tajori. 'It's fifty kilos. Not the sort of thing one carries around.'

Still on the phone with my mother, I said, 'Why?'

'It's not there,' he said, now with real dread.

I looked hard at him. That lengthy formulation, the silly pretence of not knowing the Hindi word for safe, when it was a famous word from the movies, and the absurd suggestion that my mother would take a fifty kilo safe with her to Calcutta – on what level exactly was this stupidity operating? He could not have expected me to believe the surface stupidity. But did he perhaps imagine that I would think that only someone truly very stupid would try to fool me in this way? Would I then be convinced of a deeper stupidity within him? Was I? Or did I believe that someone not in fact so stupid was making me lose myself in these double considerations? And then there was this business of him having discovered the safe's absence, unprompted, within seconds of my telling him to search the house.

Its disappearance meant many things at once: for one it was no longer a small theft; and two, Sati was no longer a suspect, not at least for having left the night before with a bag. He could have concealed two laptops in a bag, not a safe. Because of the weight of the safe it meant also that more than one person would have had to be present, which suggested planning. And since the thief seemed to have known where he was going, it suggested an inside man; most alarmingly for me, it meant the thieves had walked past my unlocked bedroom door. Their footsteps would have been heavy, I could have woken easily and if I had . . . But there was something else: an inside job meant the thieves would have known I was home. And as both my mother and I were away a lot, and the thieves would have had many opportunities to enter the house when no one was home, it not only meant that they knew I was home, they wanted me home.

'It's Kalyan for sure!' my mother said. 'How could he have known it was gone? I only just mentioned it to you. If anything, he should have been looking to see if the silver was there. He ought not even to have known about the safe. I've had my suspicions about him for a while. And he's a fool so he would give himself away like this.'

To understand her attitude, as well as the deeper tensions that would reveal themselves, it is important to say something about Kalyan's and my mother's relationship. It gives a view into the kind of half-humanity we were all living by, the small kindnesses, the resulting expectations, and now, the great disappointment and distrust.

The trouble between my mother and Kalyan began when Kalyan's little son broke his arm some six months before. It had happened in their village in Pauri Garhwal, in the mountainous state of Uttarakhand, and the village doctor who set the arm had set it badly. It began to heal crookedly and the boy was in danger of never having full use of it again. That was when Kalyan, without informing my mother, brought the boy down to Delhi. He showed him to a few doctors in the suburb of Najafgarh, close to our house, who told him that the boy's arm would have to be reset. And it would be expensive. It was at that stage that Kalyan approached my mother with a request for money. She, more irritated by the substandard medical treatment the boy had received than by the request, got Robin on the job. Robin was the highly efficient factotum – presently on his way to Steeple Hall – who worked in Sethia Coal. The boy was taken to Max Clinic, a place of cemented car parks, lush gardens and glittering green glass. And it was there, among air-conditioned pharmacies, abstract art and uniformed staff gliding smoothly over a chequered floor, that I met him for the first time.

He was swimming in the hospital's green oversized frock, and playing happily with the reclining function on the bed. He had bright black eyes full of mischief and a twinkling smile. When the doctors would give him an injection, he would dare them to give him another. They said that they had never seen a child as fearless as him. With time, his arm healed, speeded along by the incentive of a red truck my mother had promised him. On full recovery he moved in with his mother to Steeple Hall. I would see him in the evenings that followed, pedalling about on his red truck, yelling 'Namaste!' and precariously bringing his palms together in greeting.

Some months later he started school in Delhi and was joined by his sisters. My mother at first welcomed the family's arrival, feeling that they would be a grounding influence on Kalyan. But no more than a few months after they arrived, she began to feel that the opposite was true. Kalyan became careless about his work; the quality of his cooking declined; his expenses soared; one month alone his rations rose to thirty thousand rupees, almost double what she paid in Calcutta. (And this in a house that was empty for most of the month!) His quarters, big spacious rooms, he kept in squalor, allowing dirt to encrust and that sweet musty servants' smell, here infused with stale cigarettes, there with unwashed bedclothes, to pervade the place. Running alongside this visible decline were my mother's disappointed expectations of the relationship, which were like a denial of the realities of domestic servitude in India: a fond feeling that it need not be different from its incarnations in the West; that they were not really servants, as we knew them, but staff or, better still, 'help'.

But they were servants; and, by the time the theft occurred, Kalyan had been told to move his family off the property. He had looked around in the neighbourhood but soon despaired at seeing that the accommodation was small, unhygienic and often without electricity. 'Now he's finding out,' my mother would say. The night before the theft, Kalyan had brought his family back to Delhi. He housed them secretly in his quarter, despite my mother's clear instructions not to; and it was well known that even without this latest transgression Kalyan had been in danger of losing his job.

I defended him now for reasons I was barely conscious of. Was it his physical nearness to me? Did I want to think of the thief as someone living at a remove from me, and not the person who moments ago had been the first to enter my room? Or was it my belief in his talent as a cook that had led me to form an idea of his goodness as a man? Perhaps. For truly he was the most natural cook I ever met. In his hands, the ingredients of a recipe, like colours in the hands of a skilled painter, would run to meet one another. Just the day before I had watched him work on a recipe for Zack's gazpacho. One could almost hear his mind sift through each ingredient. And though some, like extra virgin olive oil, were new to him, he arrived instinctively at the right idea of proportion. He'd never seen or tasted gazpacho, but just from looking at it he was able to tell that the oil had fallen short; and with no prompting from me, added two fingers more. Then tasting it, he guessed the last two ingredients: a spoonful of salt, and a splash of non-balsamic vinegar. Watching him, I had a thought that was like a forerunner of what was to come: it would have been different elsewhere. In another country, with another idea of human possibility, Kalyan would have been a different man.

But defending him to my mother now, it was irritating to see him run through a charade of opening and shutting cabinets under the television set, which we both knew contained nothing but old VHS tapes and yellowing legal papers.

'Stop it,' I snapped, 'would the thieves have stolen the safe and laptop only to hide them in those cupboards?'

My mother chuckled down the line.

'No,' he said, looking up, 'I was just checking to see if anything else was missing.'

'Well, don't check there. There's nothing of value there. Check to see if the silver is still here.'

He went off.

I asked my mother what had been in the safe.

'Well fortunately,' she said, 'less than what was there a few weeks ago when your cousin was getting married. If they had taken it then, it would have been mega. More than one C worth. But because I had just brought most of it to Cal for appraisal there was only a few lakhs of stuff in there: a gold chain, a pair of solitaires, two Bulgari tops, that Bulgari ring I used to wear, you know the one with yellow and blue topazes. And a few old things your nani grudgingly gave me, perhaps the only things to survive our poor days in London.'

I listened and after a pause said, 'Now what?'

'Now we wait. Robin's on his way. He says we have to make a police case. In the meantime, why don't you try speaking to Kalyan. Explain to him that if he fesses up now, there'll be less trouble. He'll have to go of course – they may all have to – but there'll be less trouble with the police. Once it's in their hands they're in charge.'

Robin, the Sethia Coal factotum, was a slim man with a placid, youthful face and a thatched head of hair, whitening at the roots. He had a grave, slightly furtive manner, which came, I felt, from forever operating beyond the system. In his whispered, persuasive way, he had gained airport access equal only to that of the country's two or three most powerful fix-it men; he could arrange airline tickets when flights were twice and three times over-booked; and, on one occasion, when Amit Sethia's sister was in hospital, in need of blood, and even the city's blood banks were at a loss as to how they would find it, Robin organized a donation campaign via text message, supplying two and three times as much blood as her veins could take. 'Bas, nothing,' he said self-effacingly, when once I asked him what the secret to his influence was. 'I keep good relations with everybody. I try figuring out what each man wants – some want money, some a favour in return, some just want to speak to an honest, straightforward guy – and I adapt myself accordingly.' It was in this ability to be every man, of which the ability to look like every man was just an expression, that his true genius lay. He was the most bendable unbending man I ever knew!

His arrival at Steeple Hall made real the morning's theft. The safe and laptops, which had only been missing up to that point, became stolen items within seconds of his entry on the scene. And attaching to these stolen things were suspects, theories, points of entry, CCTV cameras and police on the way.

He stood outside, in a violet shirt and jeans, a blue tooth device in his ear, tensely surveying the scene. The property's pink buildings, blue and white awnings and its pruned springy hedges were reflected in the silver of his sunglasses. Sati had also just driven in on his moped; Kalyan had returned from searching the house, claiming nothing else was missing; and the security had finished searching the servants' quarters.

In this unprofitably altered environment, with the threat of police now at hand, the heat and dazzle of the

July day ascendant, Robin introduced a new hope. He telephoned the property's recently hired manager and told him to come quickly to unlock his office so that we could check the camera footage from the night before. The cameras! I had forgotten about them.

Kalyan, in the meantime, recounted his version of the morning's events, stopping between questions to take audible gulps of air. He had come in by the front door at 5.30 a.m. He was surprised to find it slightly ajar, but then seeing everything else in the house in its correct place, he thought nothing of it, thought perhaps that I might have left the door open while letting out Oscar (the house dog) the night before. Then Kalyan said he went into the kitchen, prepared the tea tray and brought it up to my room. Afterwards, he had gone downstairs and begun to dust in my mother's study . . .

'Dusting at five-thirty . . . ?' Robin asked and looked at me.

'Six,' Kalyan asserted with a loud breath.

'Six,' Robin repeated. 'Dusting at six?'

'Yes,' Kalyan answered, 'we always prepare the study room and baba's office at that time. Then we dust the rest of the house afterwards.'

I confirmed this was true and Kalyan continued.

'When I entered the study, I noticed that the laptops were missing. But thinking perhaps that baba was using them, I said to myself I'll ask him when he comes down.'

'Both? You thought I'd be using both the laptops, plus my third?' I asked.

'Yes,' Kalyan replied, 'so when you came down the first thing I did was to go up to your room and see if they were there. When they weren't I came down and asked you about it.'

'And the safe? How did you know to look for it so quickly?'

Kalyan paled.

'When you told me to search the house for anything else that was missing, I went up to madam's room. I saw her cupboard doors were open and the safe gone.'

'But you knew it was there?'

'Yes,' Kalyan answered after a pause, 'we all did. The cupboard doors stayed open. We put her dry-cleaned saris in the cupboard. We dusted there. We all knew it was there.'

'Who's we all?' I asked.

'Dheeraj,' Kalyan began and then stalled. Dheeraj was the bearer and Kalyan's brother-in-law; he had been on holiday since the middle of June.

'Amit?' Robin asked, introducing a new and dangerous element. He was the old manager, sacked recently under strained circumstances.

'Yes,' Kalyan replied.

'And Santosh?' Robin asked.

Santosh was one of the gardeners.

'Yes, probably,' Kalyan said again.

Robin looked up at me.

After a brief conference alone, we gave the security, Sati and Kalyan my mother's warning: if they knew anything, they should speak now and there was still a chance of the matter being settled privately. Once the police arrived, their investigation would take its course.

When they said they had no more to tell us, I said to Robin, in a voice loud enough for them all to hear, 'Never mind. The cameras will reveal everything.'

Fighting the morning's intrusion, I sought comfort in the chrysalis of my old routine. But within minutes, I sensed Robin's slim figure hovering impatiently in a dark corner of the basement study. He had, with Kalyan's assistance, found the point of entry. He took me first to the front door to show me that it couldn't be opened from the outside without a key. He trailed a finger along its edge to further show that it had in no way been forced. Then he led me to the glass and gauze doors on the other side of the house, past the kitchen and drawing room. Here, he pointed to the edge of the door's black metal frame. There was a flaking silver abrasion, as if made by a screwdriver, and bright in the morning light, at exactly the point where the handle met the frame; near it bits of black plastic were torn and hanging off.

'He entered from here,' Robin said. Sati and Kalyan had gathered around. Sati put his hand forward to touch the handle as if from wonder.

'Don't!' I said, the thought occurring to me for the first time. 'They'll need to check it for fingerprints.'

'He entered from here,' Robin repeated, 'took what he wanted and then left from the front door.'

Now Sati couldn't control himself. He fingered the door handle with sensual pleasure. I slapped his hand away. Looking up at me, he said, 'People have been touching it all morning.'

'Fine. But if your fingerprints are on it when the police arrive, you know where you're going.'

He liked this and laughed.

'They're family men,' Jasbir Singh Jat (ASI) said, 'they wouldn't have done it. Rehan saab,' adding with aplomb, 'ghar ka bhedi, Lanka dhai!' It was a reference to the grandest inside job of all time: Ravana's brother, Vibhis-hana, helping Ram to destroy Lanka. And no sooner had he discovered that Kalyan was from Uttarakhand, and not local, than he was sure he was our Vibhishana.

'There's no telling he's even Indian; in many cases they turn out to be Nepali. By the time you figure out who it is, they're back across the border.' Then looking at Kalyan, he said, 'Son, you don't eat the salt of a house and then betray the owner.'

'No, sir,' Kalyan said, beginning to tremble, the reference to salt perhaps especially close to his heart.

Jat smiled. 'Then help us,' he said.

'Sir, you're the police.'

'Yes, but that doesn't mean we pull answers out of thin air. We need your cooperation. Tell me, who did it?'

'Sir . . .'

Jat laughed, and turning to me, said, 'What was in the safe?'

'Just some jewellery belonging to my mother.'

'Money?'

'No, just jewellery.'

'Can I speak to mata ji?'

'Sure,' I said and walked over to the telephone. Above

it, hung a garlanded picture of my recently dead grandmother in floral chiffon and pearls. On the sideboard, a
framed photograph of my mother's marriage to Amit
Sethia in Phuket some years before. And next to the
telephone, a statue of Mahishasur Mardini. My eye was
trailing the shaft of the trident being plunged down the
throat of a demon when my mother's voice answered. I
explained that Jat wanted to speak to her and handed the
receiver to him.

In the minute or so that he spoke to her he grew
animated. 'Ghar ka bhedi, Lanka dhai,' he repeated,
adding also, 'now that the snake has appeared, its path
will become clear.'

My fear that my mother would help to incriminate
Kalyan turned out to be real. It was not that she wanted
an innocent man to go to prison, but her mind was
impatient with uncertainty and hurried towards a solu-
tion. Also things might have seemed clearer to her from
a distance. Whatever the cause, she not only turned
suspicion toward Kalyan, she supplied Jat with a new
theory: she believed the safe had not been stolen the night
before but days in advance, when there was no one home.
The theft of the laptops, she felt, was only a cover. This
way Kalyan would have a strong alibi: if he was the thief,

why carry out the theft on the one night I was home, and not on any of the nights when he was in sole charge of the house?

By the time Jat had put the phone down, and the forensics team arrived, his mind was inflamed with possibilities.

The team was made up of three. There was an older man in Bata chappals, loose blue trousers and an off-white shirt. He had a pockmarked face, a greying crew cut and bore a strong resemblance to the actor Om Puri. There was another, middle-aged man, bellied and with a stout face, a thin moustache and a striped blue and yellow T-shirt. And there was a young man with thick bristly hair, deep furrowed eyebrows and an intense constricted expression. It was this last member of the team who carried the forensic briefcase consisting of brushes, silver powders and magnifying glasses, each with its place carved out in a thick bed of grey foam.

They went first to the glass and gauze door where it was believed the entry had been made. The youngest of the team stood outside in the heat, frangipani trees and a sandstone pavilion behind him, brushing the glass door with silver dust. Finding only a greasy hodge-podge of prints, he moved inside. There he met with the same result except for a single print, slightly wet on the edges.

'This is usable,' he said.

But Kalyan who, after bringing the forensics experts glasses of water stood around watching, confessed that it was his, made only seconds before.

Robin's eyes fixed him in a cold stare. 'Even after baba told Sati not to touch the door, you touched it.'

The team hurried inside to dust the table from which the laptops had been taken. The young forensics expert had barely covered one corner of the table when he looked up with dismay. 'It's been cleaned,' he said, like a child about to cry.

'No, no,' I said, 'there's been no one cleaning this morning.'

'It's been cleaned,' he said again, speaking not to me but to his colleagues.

'Kalyan!' Robin yelled.

While we waited for him to come in, the most senior in the team pressed his thumb onto the desk.

'I'll show you,' he whispered to me, as if I was doubting the utility of their profession, 'what a print looks like when it's complete.'

Kalyan entered.

'You've cleaned here,' Robin said.

'No, sir,' Kalyan replied.

'It's been cleaned,' the young expert said for the third time.

'I just ran this . . .' Kalyan rushed out of the room and returned with a rainbow-plumed duster. 'I just ran this over it.'

'So you cleaned it,' Robin said, 'you came in here, saw the laptops missing and the first thing that occurs to you is to dust the desk?'

'No,' Kalyan replied, beginning again on his involved account of how he had thought I had both laptops with me.

The forensics men were leaving the room when the elder beckoned to the youngest. 'Dust here.'

The young man did as he was told and as if by magic the silvery and alluvial contours of a full print appeared.

'This is usable!' the young man said with delight and reached for a tape from his briefcase.

The other watched him with the paternal affection of a fairytale bear before breaking the sad news to him that the print was his.

'Yours! You made it?' the junior expert said with shock at this impropriety committed by a revered elder.

'Yes,' the senior expert consoled him, 'but only to show . . .' He broke off and pointed in my direction.

The team rushed out of the room and went to the last station where prints could potentially be found. But within seconds of dusting the cupboard that contained the safe, they said in one voice 'nothing'. The middle-aged expert, pointing to a sliced sliver of clear lines, added, 'Half a print here, but it's cut off. Unusable.'

After their run through the house the team cooled off in the drawing room. Their failure had made them resentful. They needled Jat: 'So do you have any suspects?'

'The police can't pull off miracles,' he said gloomily, 'we need cooperation. No one's going to come out and say, "Sir, we stole the things, take us in." Never mind. We'll give some people the third degree, then we'll get answers.'

The senior forensics expert nodded in agreement, looking over at me. 'If you don't put pressure, how will the juice come out?'

'Yes,' Jat stressed, 'without fire, how will the food cook?'

But even as I listened to the men, speaking, as it were, in code, like television policemen, I did not grasp their

full meaning. Their clichés created an illusion of procedure. They seemed like complete people, acting out a
rehearsed role, and their conversation was so fluent that
it allowed no point of entry. It was, as with the customs
of an unfamiliar society, just to be observed. And so it
was only when they began to look expectantly in my
direction that I realized, in a sudden metamorphosis from
spectator to participant, what they were asking of me,
and how extraordinary their demand was. Extraordinary,
for it, too, could be executed as a role, played out un-
thinkingly.

The policemen wanted me to select two or three of
the ten or so men who worked at Steeple Hall for a
thrashing, for what they referred to, using a dysphemism,
as the 'third degree'.

Now, before my innocence should become my biggest
crime, I should say that I, of course, knew that all of this
existed, not only in India, but elsewhere. So what was it
that surprised me? Not the police's methods. No. It was
that I had inadvertently become complicit in their violence. That a crime had been committed, that there was
no question of my being a suspect and that the rights of
ten independent adult men had been slipped into my
hands to handle as I saw fit. And for what was about to
happen, no extra-legal measures were needed; everything

would occur within the limits of the system. One did not have to go outside the law to stray: one could stray irrecoverably within the sphere of its enforcement.

Unwanted powers had become mine, and my options were few: I could choose not to act and risk the police losing interest in the case; I could abdicate responsibility and let someone less squeamish than myself – my step-father or Robin for instance – make the decision; or I could stop fooling myself about where I lived, and instead of clinging to an idea of myself formed abroad, accept the realities of the place I was from. A line from a book about India flashed through my mind: '. . . a determination, touched with fear, to remain what I was.'

I excused myself from the drawing room and went to call my mother.

She said, when I told her what the police had asked of me, 'I've already said no rough stuff. But they have to do their investigation. Why don't you try speaking to Kalyan yourself? He's a weak sort of guy. He'll confess without having to be taken to the police station. Just tell him, "Listen, Ma says that even now if you confess . . ."'

'Yes, yes, OK.'

I put the phone down and yelled for Kalyan. He appeared in the doorway of the study. His expression, though grave, seemed to be struggling to retain its normality, as if it was just another day, and I wanted, perhaps, a cold coffee. I noticed for the first time how slim and long his fingers were, like a pianist's. I tried, by fixing my gaze on his figure, to focus my thoughts. Then I lost my nerve.

'Can I have a gazpacho?' I said at last.

He looked confusedly at me.

'You know the soup I taught you to make yesterday. Put some in a glass and give it to me. If it's not cold, add an ice cube or two.'

I could make out Jat in the doorway. He stood close behind Kalyan, almost pressing up to him, smiling. Kalyan kept his cool in the face of this playground intimidation, then turned around and went back into the kitchen, passing under Jat's arm, which was propped against the door frame. Jat said he wanted to show me something outside.

We stepped into the blaze. It forced me back for a pair of sunglasses. Through their lenses the light became like the brownish yellow light of a photograph from the 1970s. The flowers of the frangipani and the pink of the sandstone pavilion acquired the gentle tones of a seaside resort.

Jat led me to the corner of the property where the

servants' quarters were. They sat at an angle, facing away from the house. 'And they're as nice,' my mother liked to say, 'as Rehan's college suite, with a drawing room and Bombay Dyeing sheets. They will learn to live like human beings if it's the last thing I do.'

But they hadn't quite. There was still that stale, sweet servant smell I had known all my life. In one of the rooms on the lower floor, a hired chauffeur lay on a single bed watching television. Near him, on a bedside table, bringing to the room something of the feel of a motel, lay a used ashtray, car keys and money. Bright religious posters were Sellotaped to the walls.

He rose hurriedly when we came in and swung around to put his shoes on. Jat looked with dull amusement around the room, then addressing him, said, 'Why did you do it?'

His name was Ashok; his father had come from Port bin Qasim in 1947; he was dark with spectacles, and frail. But this made him smile.

'Sir, no,' he said, acting up his servility, 'where would I do it?'

Jat lost interest and went into another room containing washing machines and driers. He opened them with the feigned boredom of someone hoping for a surprise. Finding them empty, he went back outside.

'Namaste!' rang out loudly. I stepped out and saw that Kalyan's son, his palms brought together in greeting, had appeared at the top of the black metal staircase that was attached to the building's exterior. It was hard to meet his gaze. His innocence and enthusiasm, still reflecting gratitude for the green glass hospital and the red truck, was like a reminder of the people we had been till a few hours ago, the people we had set out to be.

Jat eyed the boy with prurient interest. Only days before another small boy had helped incriminate his father in his mother's murder. The TV channels had shown him in someone's arms being asked by an investigator, 'Who hung up Mummy?'

'Papa hung up Mummy,' the toddler said easily, and many times.

Jat made for the stairs and I followed him, but he gestured to me to stay where I was.

A few minutes later he came back down. We were about to leave the small cemented triangle that made up the servants' forecourt when suddenly it occurred to me that he had not shown me what he had brought me out to see. Had he been waiting for me to ask? His eyes suddenly bright, Jat pointed to the green boundary wall in front of us. More specifically he pointed to an area near the top of the eight-foot wall, which appeared to have been scuffed by the shoes of someone getting over.

'Crossing has been made, Rehan saab,' he announced.

And to complete his theory, he showed me the spot where the shards of glass that ran over the top of the wall had been removed, and where a roll of razor-wire, dislodged from its place, now hung low like a slinky.

As we walked back to the house Jat noticed a gardener in the next door property. Ashirwad. A small squat sandstone building, with rounded marble minarets, giving it the aspect of an inflatable castle. It was rarely occupied and rented out, we believed, for 'functions'. Jat waved over the gardener and spoke to him in whispered tones, before rejoining me a few moments later in the house.

A centimetre of melted ice lay over the thick orange of my gazpacho. I took a sip and marvelled at how much it tasted like the ones I had had in Spain. Robin looked at it with keen interest.

'Why do you drink this? Does it reduce cholesterol?'

'No, it's just refreshing.'

'Is there garlic in it?'

'Yes.'

'What else?'

'Cucumber, a pepper, tomatoes, olive oil . . .'

Then rising to lock the door, he said, as if our casualness was part of a new calloused exterior, 'A lot of suspicion falling on him.'

'Vinegar too, I think.'

Robin nodded politely and continued. 'First he dusts the place at six, removing all the fingerprints. I mean you see that the laptops are missing and you start dusting? Then there's this business about the safe. Why should he notice it's gone so quickly? Even before you tell him to look for it? And the open door? The security was patrolling the place, they say they went around the house some six or seven times. They never saw the door open.'

'You think he was acting alone?'

'No chance. My suspicion falls on Santosh and . . .'

'Why him?'

'Rehan, he's a very suspicious character. He has all sorts of strange connections in the area. He's forever in and out of the house. And you know when the place was being built some parts went missing.'

'What kind of parts?'

'A few door handles, some fittings, but they were the most expensive parts. Italian, I think. And everyone at that point suspected Santosh. But we didn't make too much of it at the time.'

I had seen Santosh often. He had curly hair and a round childlike face. He often handed me guavas when I walked outside, pointing to various corners of progress in an ornamental vegetable garden.

'And who else?'

'Amit, for sure Amit.'

This was the former manager.

'Do you know,' Robin continued, 'before he left he threatened madam?'

'How?'

'The security is changed every six months, not the agency, the guards; it's part of their routine. Amit suddenly tells madam not to change the guards. She explains to him that they have to be changed cyclically and you know what he says to her? "Don't change them because otherwise there might be a robbery." She said to him, "Amit, are you threatening me?"'

'What did he say?'

'What's he going to say, "No, no, madam, nothing like that." My fear, Rehan,' he said, giving me a chill, 'is that they're all involved.'

'Where's Kalyan now?' I asked.

'He's taking a round with the policeman.'

Seconds later Jat appeared in the study. His eyes danced; he was in a state of high excitement.

'Come with me,' he said with a broad grin, 'I want to show you something.'

I rose, my gazpacho still in my hand.

'You can finish that,' he said.

Jat timed the climax of his explanation with our arrival at the servants' quarters. 'When we were there earlier,' he said, 'you saw footprints in only one place, right?'

I thought back to the green wall. I remembered it scuffed in two places.

'But both on the same wall, no?'

'Yes, the same wall.'

'Well, now look,' Jat said, as we entered the shade of the servants' forecourt.

He pointed at the adjacent wall. It was nearly four feet higher than the other wall, and its glass and barbed wire were in place. But five feet from the ground, about as high as the average man could kick, were a set of fresh and dusty footprints.

'It was your cook who showed them to me,' Jat said.

'What do they mean?'

'Bas, that someone heard us discussing them and marked the wall after we left, obviously wanting to give the impression that these marks are everywhere; that they don't mean anything?'

Hearing this explanation, I felt for the first time that I could see in miniature the thinking that had gone into the bigger plan. At every step circumstances had been prepared to draw us away from our most obvious conclusions: the theft of the laptops, to distract from the safe, the main prize of the robbery; the date of the robbery to throw us off our most likely suspect: if it was him, why would he choose the one night I was home and why the night his family arrives; the point of entry presented as the forced side door of glass and gauze; if it was Kalyan, he would have used the front door; he had the key; and now, the method growing cruder, the alternative footprints on the much higher wall, and in no way suggesting a place where it could have been scaled. The plan was designed to protect the most obvious suspect by suggesting a course the most obvious suspect would not have needed to take. But now, its motivations revealed, this double deception began to work against its author, implicating the most obvious man.

We shrank from the white heat. Entering the house, I handed Kalyan my empty glass of gazpacho. He stood nervously by the kitchen door. Robin and I spoke briefly in private, then we called him into my mother's study. The courage I had found hard to muster earlier came easily now. Jat sat on a single chair in one corner of the room.

'This is your last opportunity,' I said, matter-of-factly, 'even now it's not too late to confess. But let me be clear, there's a lot of suspicion falling on you.'

'I know, sir. But I know what's true. I have no guilt on my part.'

'Kalyan, try and understand that we can't turn a blind eye to this. Someone came in here last night and walked out with over a lakh's worth of stuff. They walked past my bedroom. If, by chance, I'd woken up they would have killed me. You have to know something.'

'Sir, there are more than ten people who work here, it could have been any one of them.'

'That is not so many. There are fifteen million in the city. To find one man there, on the outside, would have been difficult. To find one in ten is not so difficult. And the police have their methods.'

Kalyan flashed a glance at Jat who looked directly ahead.

'You do concede that it's an inside job, don't you?' I continued.

'Yes.'

'So whom do you suspect?'

'Sir, I don't want to put any false accusations on

anyone. I feel so bad that this has happened. As much as this is your house, it is my house too. Madam has done so much for me. She saved my son's arm, she sent him to school, she's given me so many opportunities . . .'

'Kalyan, be careful,' Robin, seated on a bamboo stool, intervened. And building a case for his guilt out of what I knew to be nothing, he said, 'Right now, in the eyes of the police, you are not only a suspect, you are guilty of destroying evidence. First you dust the desk from where the robberies occurred, then your fingerprint appears on the glass after baba has told you explicitly not to touch anything . . .'

'Robin, sir, I was trying to avoid touching the handle. If I was the one who did it why would I choose this day of all days when baba is here? I've had the house to myself for the past fifteen days. And why the day when my family arrives?'

Robin and I looked at each other. To hear this rationale come so easily to Kalyan did more to damn him than anything we had said. The man who played stupid was not so stupid as not to have thought of an alibi. And quite a sophisticated alibi at that: one that included a moral component — would any man endanger his family? — while functioning on an inverted surely-not-the-butler logic. Already Jat was an ardent subscriber to my mother's theory that the safe had been taken on a different day. Now he intervened. Opening the soft grey file on his lap, and beckoning Kalyan over, he pointed to the first exposed sheet. Even from a distance I could see that it said in English 'Arrest Order'.

'You know what this is?'

Kalyan looked genuinely blank.

'Oh you want to see it in Hindi. Wait, bachchu, I'll show you.' He flipped through the file, nearly dropping the papers between his legs, then opened to a page, which had English and Hindi. 'It's not good to be a namak haram,' he said, 'I'll show you what we do in the station to men who eat the salt of a house and then betray its owner.' Looking at Robin and me, Jat said, 'Now leave us alone, please.'

We went out of the room.

Already polluted by the morning's emotions, my happy ideas of a summer in India ruined, my routine broken into, I felt myself a rougher man than I knew. To be morally superior in India was to feel physically weak and insecure. And, as though revisited by that childhood longing for security, I ached to feel strong, to shed any naivety that might still remain. I wanted the servants quickly to know how ruthless I could be.

The door opened. Kalyan appeared with red eyes, and with voice trembling, said, 'They're taking me away.'

The pity that arose in me turned to anger.

'No one's taking you away,' I yelled hatefully at Kalyan, pushing him inside the study, 'but you have to cooperate. You have to tell us what happened or we can't help you. Such a big robbery has happened under your nose. And you have nothing to say. What would you do if you were in my position? Pretend it didn't happen and carry on? Kalyan, you better think fast what happened or no one will be able to help you. Think of your children.'

I couldn't gauge his reaction; unused to handling these heightened emotions, I couldn't see past my own nerves and anger. Jat stepped in, sending Kalyan out of the room and gently closing the door behind him. I sank into the leather chair in front of the desk from where the laptops had gone missing. Their loss seemed so insignificant in the face of the situation that had arisen.

'Be calm, be calm,' Jat advised with a smile, 'nothing comes of force. Even in our investigations if you hit too hard too early, the suspect toughens. Then there is no way in. Play him sweet now. Tell him that you have prevented me from taking him away. Abuse us if you have to. Everyone does. Then you watch. Nothing works better on guilt than a dose of kindness administered at the right moment.'

I opened the door and the face Kalyan saw through the fingerprinted glass of the kitchen pane was a smiling one. I pushed open the swing door, and putting a cupped hand to Kalyan's cheek, said, 'I won't let anyone take you anywhere. You are our old, loyal servant. You'll stay right here. This theft will only be resolved with your help. Now hurry up, put lunch on the table.' And as I said these words, a new and soothing coolness flowed into me. I felt my transformation had begun.

That afternoon, the police, sensing a more substantial crime had been committed, sent men of high rank and caste. Leading the new command was Vijay Singh, the inspector at Chawalla police station. He was a tall well-built man in his late forties with hawkish eyes, a long face and a brief bristly moustache. Though he spoke mainly in Hindi, he would have occasional and fluent effusions in English centred on a single, admired word, such as 'systematic' or 'revive'. His rank was written into his uniform: it was pale beige, of a far better material than Jat's, and it struck an attractive harmony with the blue of his braided shoulder cord and the red and blue of the police badge. He was accompanied by Sub-Inspector

Surinder Sharma, a stout older man with hennaed hair, who had large protruding teeth that fixed his mouth in a permanent grimace. Around these men, his superiors, Jat shrank. Once imposing, he now became the station clown, sly and cruel, his humour bawdy.

Vijay Singh did a brisk inspection of the property. He was followed by a young handsome constable whose beauty was marred, as if part of the grotesque quality of the day, by a dense patch of warts, maybe fifty, at the exact point where the jaw met the neck.

After his cursory inspection, Vijay Singh confirmed that the theft was an inside job. 'The man knew exactly where he was going. An outside man wouldn't have had the balls to do this. One of your own men is eating from your hand while driving a knife into you.'

'Do you see many thefts like this?' I asked.

We stood outside the front door. In the cobbled area beyond, Singh's white Gypsy, full of women police officers in khaki salwar kurtas, waited.

'Yes, but never in a farmhouse. This is the first in a farmhouse.'

'Really, how come?'

'Because they're normally very well guarded. A farm-house,' he said, evoking their reputation as places of vice and luxury, 'is like your temple. It should be completely private. Even the police shouldn't be allowed in. You never know what might be happening in a farmhouse.'

I nodded, vaguely registering the suggestiveness of his tone.

He misunderstood my expression and it brought a smile of complicity to his face.

'You need to *revive* your security, Rehan saab,' he said, climbing into his Gypsy, 'you need to *revive* your security. Someone from within is giving you the knife.'

With this, he drove away, leaving Surinder Sharma to begin the first of the drawing-room trials. Once he had gone, Sharma become emboldened.

'Are you a Kashmiri, sir?' he asked with overfamiliarity, introducing some new regional prejudice into the mix, even though I, for being English-speaking and privileged, was in an important sense, as with the law, above these caste-, region- and faith-based judgements.

'No, Punjabi. Why?'

'Just from your dress,' he smiled, pointing at my white salwar kameez.

'It's worn in Punjab too,' I said firmly.

We sat down in the drawing room. Robin handed me a file containing the identification documents of the staff at Steeple Hall. No sooner had I started flipping through it than I felt an unexpected pang. It came from being made aware of human details – like Dheeraj's birth date, 1st of June, 1983, so twenty-two a few weeks ago; Narender the electrician's birthplace in the hill town of Almora, which I had visited as a child; and Santosh's residence, described as 'at Needou the Untouchable's, behind the petrol pump' – which one, even after a lifetime of employing people in India, never discovered about them. Servants didn't have birthdays or zodiac signs; their age and the places they had lived and grown up in didn't matter. But now, shown these documents for the first time, I thought I could see in Dheeraj's passport picture the excitement of its purpose, the anticipation of life in the big city; I was struck by the grand Hindu names from the epics, like that of Kalyan's mother, Draupadi Devi, still alive in temple-going India, but forgotten and degraded in Farmhouse Delhi; and perhaps most alarmingly of all, Time, with its special ravages on servants: Kalyan, whose age I might have put at thirty-five, was, in fact, born in 1978, just five years before me.

In Jat's hands these documents revealed a variety of regional and caste-related knowledge, which acted like evidence itself. He took the sheets and separated them into two suspect camps, the Garhwal camp from the hills of Uttarakhand, which included Kalyan, Dheeraj and

Narender, and the Delhi/Bihar camp which, led by Santosh, included the rest.

Kalyan was the first in.

Robin and I sat on one sofa, the police on two straight-backed armchairs with a table and vase containing tuber-oses between them. Sharma led the inquiry.

Taking in his entire figure at once, Sharma said, 'Kalyan, why are your legs shaking?'

Kalyan looked down at them as if they were somebody else's legs. 'No, sir, they're not.'

Sharma reached forward and fingered the fabric of Kalyan's pale-blue trousers.

'Never mind,' he said after a pause, and smiled. 'I thought they were. I might have been mistaken. How long have you been working here?'

'It must be three and a half years, sir.'

'Three and a half years. What do you earn?'

'Four and a half thousand.'

'Four and a half thousand, but you wanted more?'

It took a moment for Kalyan to gauge his meaning.

'No, no . . .' he sputtered.

Sharma and Jat smiled at each other. They had a surprise for him. Sharma fingered the cuff of his rolled-up shirt while Jat spoke.

'You told us you knew no one in the area?' Jat said.

'I don't,' Kalyan replied and gulped noisily.

'But what about Dinesh?'

Kalyan's face lost all colour.

Speaking among themselves, one of the policemen said to the other, 'Have you searched his quarters?'

'Yes, yes, I even spoke to his wife.'

'Haan, so tell us, Kalyan?' Sharma said, picking up where Jat had left off. 'When did your friendship with Dinesh begin?'

Kalyan, recovering himself, said, 'He's just a guy I sometimes meet. There's no friendship.'

'But he's also from Pauri Garhwal, isn't he?'

'Yes,' Kalyan replied.

Unable to contain myself, I said, 'From the same village?'

'No, no,' Kalyan replied, looking at me, 'not the same village. I met him here for the first time.'

'How far away?' Sharma said, cautioning me to be quiet.

'Fifteen kilometres or so.'

'So not too far,' Sharma stressed. He had, after fingering Kalyan's shirt, worked his way into the pockets of his trousers. He now removed from them, a mobile phone, a packet of chewing tobacco and a soft black leather wallet, which fell open to reveal a picture of his son in the red truck my mother had given him. The probing cruelty with which these personal articles were revealed was, as with the details of his life, at once humanizing and degrading.

Sharma's hands now worked their way up Kalyan's shirt, one finger digging into a small hole on the front.

'How did you get this?' Sharma said.

'Tore it on the wall?' Jat pressed.

Kalyan, seeming almost to laugh from nerves, said, 'No, sir. It's been there for ever.'

'What about these creases on your shirt? Were these the same clothes you were wearing when you discovered the laptops?'

The two questions had been positioned in such a way that Kalyan had to pick his way out of their implications.

'I'm wearing what I was wearing last night,' he said at last.

'I see,' Sharma said, 'and were you wearing your trousers up to your nipples?'

'Sorry?'

'How did you get these bloody creases, you fool?' Jat barked.

Sharma gestured for calm with the gentle fanning of his folder.

'Kalyan, do you drink?'

Kalyan paused, and seeming to make a calculation, said, 'Sir, yes. Why lie? I do.'

'Beer or spirits?'

'Both.'

'Cards?'

'No.'

'Do you drink alone or with someone?'

'Alone.'

'Are you sure?'

'Yes.'

'How much?'

'Three or four times a week?'

This surprised me; I didn't think of him as a drinking man. And without forming any considered judgement, the police's morality made an impression on me.

'Did you drink the night of the theft?'

Now there was a notable silence and an audible gulp. 'Yes,' Kalyan replied.

'What? Whisky?'

'No, sir, rum.'

'Why rum?' Sharma asked with genuine interest.

'It's cheaper, sir, and readily available at the BSF canteen.'

The BSF was the Border Security Force; they had a base opposite our house.

'So, Kalyan,' Sharma said, 'you drank in front of your family.'

'No, not in front of them. I put the peg into a steel glass and downed it with my dinner.'

'Downed it with your dinner,' Sharma repeated, blandly adding, 'and came back to take the safe. Bastard.'

It was clear from their method of parroting insignificant details, the deliberate changes in the tone and their studied mixture of boredom and cruelty that they had had training. But they were finished with Kalyan. This was a preliminary investigation, just a way to flush out conflicting stories and spread panic among the confederates.

Sati was in next. He was calm and aloof throughout. He stood in the middle of the room, his large paunch on display and his prominent lips half-open as if in contempt. He recounted with ease the previous night's closing up. If the police became too familiar, now enquiring into his drinking habits, now asking how he fitted the safe into his night bag, he would pause and look at them with adult disdain. 'It's not him,' Sharma said at last. And it wasn't; I was embarrassed for him even to be questioned; he'd been with us eight years. But before walking out, he left us with a detail. His night bag was full because on the way to work he had bought mangoes for his son.

When he was leaving at night it occurred to him that perhaps Kalyan's children would want a few. He took three or four out, put them in a cloth with ice and both the men walked over to the quarter where Kalyan's family had just arrived, after their ten-hour bus journey from the hills. And it was these details completing the picture of Kalyan's evening, of rum in a steel glass and children eating mangoes, the light and noise of a television in the background, that made it impossible for me to think of him as the thief.

But everyone had their details. Santosh, standing before us in a tight striped T-shirt and flared jeans, had his.

'Where do you live?'

'At Needou the Untouchable's.'

'The Untouchable!' Jat said. 'We can't write that. Just write Needou.'

'How long have you been with madam?'

'Since childhood,' Santosh replied.

This was blatantly untrue.

'You've been with her since childhood?' the police asked, and looked over at me.

I shook my head.

'Not with her,' Santosh replied, 'but on the property. I was born here and worked for the previous owners.'

'Ah!' Jat said. 'You mean to say you were given as part of the dowry.'

Everyone chortled.

Jat, suddenly serious, said, 'How's that girl you've been fucking? You know the one I saw you with.'

Santosh looked at him with a puzzled smile, dimples appearing in his cheeks. He tried shrugging off the question as if it were the lewd joke of a friend.

'Sir, what girl? I've just got married.'

Robin confirmed that this was true. He had been married only the month before. And this to me, as with the description of Kalyan with his family the previous night, was like proof of his innocence. But the police were unmoved.

'So? When's that ever stopped anyone?' Jat said. 'And your friend,' he added now somewhat lamely, 'didn't I see you with him on the day there was a fire in Bijwasan?'

Santosh, now bolder, smiled with open disregard at Jat.

The police ran through their standard morality test: Drink? Beer, and that too very occasionally. Cards? Never. Parties? Never. Hookers? Sir, I'm newly married.

'And do you know Dinesh?'

'Only from the times when he would come to see Kalyan?'

'Oh. You were present on these occasions?'

'I was not present. I just knew about them.'

'How did you know about them without being present?'

'Just. You know, sir. One finds out. From the guards and people like that?'

Robin: 'Why were the guards telling you if Kalyan had guests or not?'

Sharma fanned his folder at Robin to say 'allow me'.

'And when was the most recent of these occasions?'

'Just a few months ago. It was a party to celebrate Dheeraj's wedding.'

'A party? Was there alcohol?'

'Yes, there was.'

'Beer or spirits?'

'Both.'

'Girls?'

'No, sir.'

'And were you present? Or did you know about it from the guards?'

'I just came in and out.'

'Had a glass of beer perhaps?'

'No, sir.'

'Are you listening, Mr Rehan, to what happens in your house when you're not here.'

I was not only listening; I was full of indignation. But at what exactly? That a few grown men had had a celebration in their quarters that involved alcohol? Where was the harm in that? What had they done that I wouldn't do myself? Once more, I came up against my undeclared expectations of servitude, which was really an expectation of a kind of subdued humanity. Just as servants didn't have birthdays, so I was now surprised they had parties. Not surprised; offended.

Santosh was sent out and another gardener came in. He was small and very dark with a bird-like frame. His eyes were wide with alarm and sunken, his hair thick and springy. He wore his dirty beige shirt out and removed his smoothly worn Bata slippers before stepping onto the carpet. His feet were hard and calloused.

'What are your duties?' Surinder Sharma asked.

'I am one of the gardeners.'

'Do you ever come inside the house?'

'Yes, to water the plants.'

'Do you go to all the rooms in the house?'

'Yes,' the gardener replied.

'And how many are there?' Surinder Sharma asked cryptically.

'This, I don't know,' the man replied, as if already being asked to consider an impropriety.

'You go to all the rooms in the house, but you don't know how many there are? Very strange. What is in the rooms?'

'Sir, I just water the plants. I don't know.'

'Yes, but you have eyes, don't you? If I come into this room, for instance, I can see that there are sofas, some tables, a few silver frames. I don't need anybody to tell me.'

The gardener made no reply. But I could tell he was not lying. His way of looking was not like Sharma's. I had seen him at his work. He went from station to station with his pale-brown pipe in coils around his shoulder. I believed him when he said he saw nothing else, that he hadn't even considered how many rooms there were in the house. His business was the plants and he went about it blindly; it was all he knew. And this was another shade of the crime: it was like a crime of looking, of seeing more than one's position permitted. I could see also that what I had thought was morality in the police's questioning was not in fact morality. They were trying to establish, though perhaps unaware of it, the audacity of the suspect's way of looking: what he was capable of seeing, and by extension, of coveting. And they were right to ask about gambling, alcohol and women. Because though these things were not all, they gave an indication of what a man had seen in his life and the values he had given up to see them. The police wanted to know what temptations each man had succumbed to, and the desires that still lay buried in him. Then, by divining the secrets of this heart that had dared to desire beyond its station, they would ferret out the thief that resided in it.

'Where do you live, mali?' Sharma continued.

'In the Harijan colony.'

'Are you a drinking man?'

'No, sir. I don't touch the stuff.'

'You look like a drinking man. I can tell by your face that you drink.'

I could see what Sharma meant. The yellowing eyes. The dark unhealthy· skin stretched like leather over the small bones of his face. But it could just as easily have been a caste assumption or an aspect of poverty and undernourishment.

'Sir, no,' the gardener insisted, then resorting to the ultimate Gandhian virtue, added, 'I am a poor man.'

'Now you're not!' Sharma said and everyone guffawed.

The last in was the sweeper. He was slightly made with pale skin and good features. He was also attentive to his toilette and dress. He wore a fashionable close-fitting T-shirt and jeans; a carefully shaved goatee framed his prominent lips and clean white teeth. Marring this generally pleasing impression were the hard and inflamed beginnings of a huge boil on his cheek, a boil that was yet to unleash its fury.

When the policemen discovered he was the sweeper, their tone changed from subtle and playful, to outright violent. They seemed close to hitting him just for being in their presence. He answered their stock questions in a whine. His jaw was clenched, the teeth clamped shut, as if out of the discomfort caused by the boil. He answered with painful innocence.

Was he married?

No.

Why?

He was still young.

What did he earn?

Two thousand a month.

But he didn't think that was enough. Had he thought he might help himself to a raise?

At the mention of a raise an expression of hopefulness entered his face. 'A raise would be a great help,' he said.

'A raise would be a great help,' Jat imitated in a whining voice. 'Get out you bloody idiot before I thrash you.'

It was late afternoon when the last of the drawing-room trials ended. The policemen, though they seemed no nearer to solving the case, were satisfied. They now readily accepted our offer of food and drink. Presently a plate of sandwiches, followed fast by a second, arrived, and the men, with the plate between them, wolfed down a dozen, dipping them heavily in a pool of ketchup. They would sometimes pause, and with mouths full say, 'See, Mr Rehan, what you've learnt about your house today.'

At five, another strange message from Zack: 'Deeply disturbed by events in London. Hope you didn't know anyone. Don't fall into easy attitudes.'

As evening fell I found I didn't want to be alone. The house tried brokenly to recover its routine, but it was a place now suspicious of itself. And outsiders were a comfort. As Robin sorted through plastic boxes full of keys – three sets for each glass and gauze door, of which there were as many as ten – finding some missing and others unaccounted for, I called a cousin and asked him to come over and spend the night. He agreed but said it would take him a few hours.

In the meantime, Vijay Singh returned with an officer of still higher rank. I hadn't thought that the interplay of caste and heraldry could become more refined. But Prakash Shourie wore a uniform of a still sleeker material than Vijay Singh's. He had three stars on his epaulettes, ribbon-bar slides in rich oranges and browns and a braided shoulder cord of Prussian blue; his tan leather shoes shone brightly. And though an older man, bellied and balding, I saw in his paler and softer skin the high features of a Brahmin. His fluency in English far surpassed that of Vijay Singh. He spoke in an unbroken stream, disapproving and dismissive, quizzing me on the details of the case, as if he were a doctor chastening a young patient for contracting an STD. He was also a man of clichés. 'While cat's away rats will play,' he said with relish when he heard we did not spend much time at the farm.

In minutes he demolished the point-of-entry theory, which now Robin confessed had been Kalyan's. Walking briskly up to the glass and gauze door, he demonstrated that the abrasion on the frame had not been made by a tool, but by the handle of the door's lock brushing against the frame. Then once he had shown us to be deserving of burglary, and inept at solving crime, he no longer wished to talk of the theft. He wanted instead to know where my mother's practice was; was she really the Udaya Singh whose legal victories he had read about in the eighties? Was Amit Sethia, the industrialist, my father? When I said 'stepfather' he asked, 'And your father?'

'Abroad.' The interest drained from his face.

Surinder Sharma had joined us and in the presence of his superiors, he became, as Jat had before him, a lesser man, a source of fun and suggestive humour. 'Sir, Mr Rehan, sir, speaks very lovely Punjabi,' he said, throwing upward glances at Shourie and exposing his faintly green-capped teeth.

'And so?' Shourie replied with a stern smile. 'We're all Punjabis.' At this Sharma laughed and bowed as if some important observation had been made.

Only when the senior officers had left did he become his normal self. We stood outside smoking in the growing darkness; the heat, now without its source, had a magical intensity.

'My suspicion,' he said, 'falls a hundred per cent on the cook and Santosh. We just have to find some way to get it out of them. Chalo, let's see. We'll take them in for remand,' he added as if it were a procedure in itself.

'Nothing too rough, please,' I said, the new role coming easily.

'No, no. These days there's a lot of scrutiny on our methods so we can't do anything too bad anyway.'

'What kind of scrutiny?'

'Bas, you know, human rights nonsense.' At this he laughed deeply. Then he made an absurd suggestion. 'Why don't you organize a party for these guys with alcohol? Once they're all talli, they will, by themselves only, start talking and showing off about what they've done.'

'Well, naturally, I couldn't be present at such a party.'

'No, no, naturally.'

'So how will I know what they talk about?'

Surinder Sharma looked despairingly at me, as if I had poked a hole in an otherwise excellent plan.

'You don't have a man on the inside?' he said.

'No,' I replied, feeling now in the face of this abysmal stupidity, all the futility of the day's violence and cruelty.

That night Kalyan was full of nerves.

My cousin had arrived, the lamps in the drawing room had been lit, Begum Akhtar was playing off an iPod in some further room. On the bar, a silver ice bucket had misted over, an open bottle of Famous Grouse lay mostly undrunk and, in a clear carafe of soda, bubbles fired to the surface.

I was on my way to the kitchen, when I heard a small girl's voice yell, 'Papa, papa.' It sounded like one of Kalyan's girls, but as I had never seen them in the main house before, I wasn't sure. My entry into the kitchen coincided with hers. She saw me and her eyes showed white; she clutched at the little white frock she wore.

Kalyan, standing with his back to me, seemed not to have noticed me come in. But the sight of the girl sent him into a rage. The veins in his neck swelled. He began hoarsely screaming at her to go back to the quarters. The girl, as though physically struck by her terror, vanished. It was then that Kalyan swivelled around and saw me.

The light from the stove fell over a pot of dal coming slowly to a boil and a pool of sunflower oil heating in a smooth black pan. On the granite counter, in a pink heap of freshly cut onions, there was a knife, its brushed steel surface belying the sharpness of its blade.

'What's the matter, Kalyan?'

He turned the heat down on the stove. And with his head in his hands, he let himself drop with a groan onto a low stool.

'Kalyan, what's the matter?' I said, wishing to console him, even while my gaze remained fixed on the knife.

After many moments he looked up, his eyes bloodshot, his face drawn and haggard.

'Oh God,' he said, 'if something happens to me, what will they do?'

Suppressing a stab of emotion, I said in my firmest voice, 'Kalyan, nothing is going to happen to you or them, but there's been a big robbery. It's happened under your nose. It has to be investigated. I warned you that the police would do their job. Now pull yourself together, it isn't pleasant for me either.'

He undid his apron strings and dropped his face again.

'My children haven't eaten a thing since all of this happened,' he said, his voice indistinct. 'My wife, you should see her face.' Suddenly he rose. He turned the heat up on the stove and looked with dazed confusion at its grimy surface. The exhaust whirred. My eyes were fixed on the knife in the pile of onions.

At last he said, 'You people are like gods to me. I know that what madam has done for my family no one else would have done. This is your house, but it's my house too. You can't imagine how awful I feel that on my watch this robbery has happened.'

'Well, then, you must do something to help.'

'There are at least ten people who work here . . .'

'Stop saying that! I said before that is not so many.'

'There is a new manager.'

'Are you saying that you have some doubt about him?'

'No, I'm just saying that he's new. We don't know anything about him. And you know Robin, sir, he thinks he's taken all the keys, but there are keys missing. He doesn't have all the keys.'

'What do you mean, Kalyan? Why didn't you say something earlier?'

'I just thought of it. And Amit still has the keys to his office. He never gave them up.'

The manager's office was a separate structure from the main house. But it contained all the keys. Anyone with access to it would have access to all the house's entrances.

'Somebody did not do this,' Kalyan said cryptically, 'somebody had this done.'

I felt that at any minute I was about to hear a confession. But I was too perturbed to receive it. Not with that knife lying there and Kalyan's manner so changeable.

'Kalyan,' I said at last, moving back, 'if you know something, now is the time to say it. It is not too late. The theft we would forgive. It's the truth that is important. No one will harm you or your family. You have my word.'

But if earlier he had been close to cracking, he now recovered his composure. He had no idea who had done this terrible thing. But he would do everything he could to help the police. More than anyone it was him who wanted to find the man, this man who had laid the most terrible of all traps for him – and him alone – to fall into. Hearing him speak, I felt again the possible truth of his words. After all, since it was almost definitely a collaboration, why would he volunteer himself for something that would put him in so precarious a position, with so much to lose? And why, even if the safe had not been taken the day before, force everything to its crisis on the day your family arrives in town?

But the day was not done. And, when I went back into the drawing room I had an indication of how consuming and surreal it had been: my cousin, sipping his whisky soda, said, 'I can't believe the blasts in London.'

'What blasts?' I asked, realizing even as I spoke, what Zack's text message had meant.

*   *   *

Saturday. No gardeners or sweepers were allowed into Steeple Hall. An unnatural calm fell over the place. At eleven there was a video. The camera footage of Friday night. The new manager had not been able to retrieve it until now. Four or five of us – Robin, the manager, my cousin, Sati and Narender, the electrician – sat in the manager's office watching. The little room with its small ceiling fan and windows thrown open, the red gravel of the drive all around, baked. It was impossible to think of the manager spending whole days in here.

The screen was divided into four segments, of which two were useless from our point of view: one camera had been focused on an unlit part of the garden; the other, though full of the drama of headlights hurtling through the night, as in a David Lynch movie, looked onto the road outside. We watched the other two segments, from a camera trained on the drive and another on the front door, riveted. Their electronic gaze accentuated the stillness of the night. The white path-lights in the distance seemed to pulsate. Partially concealing one camera's view was the buoyant canopy of an *Alstonia scholaris*. When the wind went through the tree, bringing some rare movement before the stillness of the camera's eye, we all sat up, expecting any minute for the front door to open and figures to emerge carrying out the safe. But the night deepened and the stillness remained. We seemed also to be watching highlights rather than the entire film. Narender, the electrician, said that the cameras were motion-activated. And this made sense, he pointed out, as we could hardly have sat there for the full twelve hours.

Sati, watching with morose fascination, asked, 'But how can they differentiate between the movement of a tree and the movement of a person?'

Narender had no answer. And already by 10 p.m. we could see there was a flaw in his theory: the cameras had not caught me letting out Oscar. Nor had they once caught the guards doing their rounds. This was less easily explained. Because even if the cameras, perhaps not activated by movement, had missed the twenty seconds in which I let out Oscar, they could not have missed, despite their abridged vision, each of the several rounds the guards claimed to have made.

'Unless they're lying,' Robin said, 'unless they did no rounds.'

The timer at the bottom of the screen read 2 a.m.

'This is the time,' the manager muttered, 'if we see anything, we'll see it now, between two and three.'

I thought of myself sleeping in the darkened house and felt a chill, felt as if I was watching myself through other eyes, and with malice. The tension in the room was high. At one point Kalyan tried to come in with bottles of water.

'Get out, get out,' Robin barked at him as if his presence in the room would erase the footage.

Wishing to lighten the air, I said, 'Sati, have you ever watched a movie where nothing happens, this intently?'

'Sir,' he replied, 'I didn't even watch my marriage video this intently.'

But by four, when in an abrupt jolting movement, the sky began to lighten, it became clear that we would see nothing. At five the screen, which I had thought was black and white, filled with colour – the green of the garden and trees, the pink of the house, the red of the drive. At six the guards, their faces still sodden with sleep, did their first rounds.

'Can you believe it?' Robin said. 'Now they're starting their rounds!'

The disappointment of what the cameras had not seen caused the net of suspicion to widen. The guards had deliberately not patrolled that night; Amit had been the mastermind; Kalyan and Santosh were promised a share; the safe had been thrown over the boundary wall to Dinesh, who had possibly buried it on the neighbouring property; since in all likelihood the robbery of the safe had occurred before the robbery of the laptops, Dheeraj, as Kalyan's brother-in-law, might also have been involved.

The other element in the equation to turn variable was the actual value of what was stolen. My mother, every few hours, was remembering a new piece of jewellery that had been in the safe. And with every addition, for instance a set of champagne pearls with an uncut diamond – a present from Amit Sethia – the loss swelled by lakhs.

Her pain at what had been lost became keener when she considered that the great part of her jewellery's value lay in the people who had made it, jewellers such as Bulgari and Cartier. But this aspect of their value had no importance in India and would have meant nothing to the people who stole it. In fact it was fair to say that only a handful of jewellers in the entire country were capable of assessing the jewellery's value in these terms. And it was not to these places that the thieves would go. Where they would go, the jewellery would be broken up like scrap metal into gold and precious stones and sold piecemeal. And in this form, now with irony spread evenly among victims and culprits, it was not really worth much. My mother could not manage a smile at the philosophical implications of this: the special pain of losing the things into which we breathe hidden value; and India, ever prepared to cut down to size anyone clinging to alien refinements. No, she was pissed off and full of bitter sadness.

That night Kalyan's family, having made the twelve-hour bus journey from Pauri Garhwal only twenty-four hours before, were sent home. My stepfather felt that if Kalyan was to be arrested it was better his family were not there. The thought of their arrival, full of expectation at seeing their father and the big city, set now against this tainted departure, was heartbreaking. I had to stop myself from thinking of their disappointment and fear on that same Uttarakhand Roadways bus, heavy with the smell of diesel, coiling its way back through unlit mountain roads to the place from where it came. I felt an irrational anger at my stepfather and mother for exposing me to this image. I knew very well that Kalyan's guilt would not be enough to erase it. This was not the kind of impression that could be reasoned away. A strange thought, like a lament for the man I had been in another place, entered my mind. I thought, if India was the sort of country where college essays were written about such things, Kalyan's son might grow up to write one about this visit to the capital. A Day in Town. The Night Bus. The Arrest. He would have all the material he needed. And where would I be in such an essay? A small player in the background, a figure of fun perhaps, denied even the dignity of a villain. A sharper eye, darkly humorous, might want to treat the question of my borrowed literary aspirations and their fraudulence, when seen against the backdrop on which they operated. One might wonder what fine sensibilities could remain in a man overseeing a week-long thrashing of at least a few innocent men, hardly older than himself?

* * *

Day three. My mother had arrived in Delhi. The gardeners and sweepers had returned to Steeple Hall and the first thrashings had begun. The police wanted to start with Santosh and work their way to Kalyan, picking up likely accomplices along the way.

On the Thursday evening after the robbery, when the sky had darkened with a dust storm, and British cities were full of police raids, I sat at the desk in my basement study. But for the pool of protective light from the banker lamp, the room was drowned in silvery obscurity. It brought a hush, making the rest of the house seem far away. Despite the silence, it was some moments before I became aware of Robin hovering in the doorway. He held a sheet of paper in his hands and his dimly visible face, as though reflecting the mood of the storm, was filled with expectation.

'Do you have a second, Rehan?'

'Yes,' I said, leaning back in my chair. Robin approached; the gloom retreated. He laid the sheet of paper in the pool of light on my desk. It was an Airtel record of calls and text messages made and received. Some numbers had a tick against them in black.

'Whose phone is this?'

'Amit's,' Robin replied. The ex-manager. He had been

dismissed at the beginning of the month. He was a small fleshy man with unhealthy skin and hooded eyes. I recalled his sly, deferential manner.

'And what are these ticked numbers?'

'Kalyan's.'

I looked up at Robin, trying to gauge his meaning. Why would it be so strange for Kalyan, the cook, to call Amit, the manager?

'Look at the date of the calls,' Robin said after a moment's pause. 'June the sixteenth, seventeenth, eighteenth. These calls were made after Amit was dismissed. They were not friends. What business did Kalyan have calling Amit repeatedly after he was sacked?'

The truth be told, Robin's suspicions made a weak impression. But he looked so furtive and the room so suggestive that I did not want to disappoint. I tried to appear as grave as I could and trailed my eye down the list of numbers. One of them, also from mid-June, showed a call of nearly fifteen minutes. 9958661273.

'What's this one?'

'I don't know.'

The suspense was growing cold when Robin said, 'Dial it.'

'What?'

'Dial it. It might be saved on your phone.'

Kinky, I thought, but why not!

I punched in the number. At first the numerals remained numerals, but just as the call connected, they morphed into a blinking name. Dheeraj! I flashed it past Robin's eyes and pressed disconnect. For a moment, Robin's face, illuminated by the white light of the phone, gleamed with intrigue.

'Come on,' he said, 'come with me to the police station.'

To witness the importance of Chawalla's main road to its village economy was to have an idea of what the river would have meant to earlier settlements. All its single-storey structures with their dusty shutters and unpainted flanks were ranged along it. The petrol pump. The temple. The chemists, chai shops and mechanics. Beyond this facsimile of every Indian village was the peach-coloured mansion, ornamented with religious symbols and reflective glass, of Shokeen, the estate agent turned politician. There was the British School, promising Cambridge-affiliated degrees and English. There was the Reliance mobile-phone shop, a sanctuary of glass and cool amid the choking traffic and diesel fumes. And on both sides, only metres past this hardscrabble stretch, clinging to the road for sustenance, were dung-filled streets with reposing buffaloes, leading directly into open fields.

On the way to the police station we passed more Shokeen land. Only months before, Robin said, he had attended the estate agent's daughter's two-crore wedding. The man, who had become a millionaire overnight from selling land to people wishing to move out of Delhi, had flown in performers from Bombay. They had arrived in a giant egg, whose shell had opened to reveal a revolving dance floor.

Just beyond, Chawalla police station was a complex of chalky pink buildings and khaki tents under the shade of a large neem tree. At the entrance there was a small open area crowded with motorbikes. Narrow mud paths lined with stunted Ashok trees led past rooms marked, 'Wireless room', 'Interrogation room', 'Loot Room' and little sandwich-size snippets of grass edged with a border of upturned bricks. Surinder Sharma, now out of uniform and in two shades of brown, greeted us at the gate.

'Welcome to my poor house,' he said, revealing his capped teeth. He led us toward the SHO's office past a khaki tent under whose scalloped hem I could make out two bare feet on the mud floor, stretched widely apart. The legs, bare too, were covered in sparse kinky hair. And though I was no longer the man I had been on Friday, not nearly so squeamish, not indeed afraid to lay plots of my own, I felt something of the horror of a child soldier, when Surinder Sharma pointed to the tent with his stick, and jumping his eyebrows, said, 'Santosh.'

'What are you having him do?'

'Oh, nothing, just stand with his legs apart. It creates,' he added, lightly trailing his fingers along the inside of his thighs, 'a burning sensation in the legs.'

'How many hours?'

'Six,' he replied uncertainly.

'Any results?'

'No, Rehan saab, this is nothing for a hardened criminal like him.' And seeing he had stirred something in me, he added, 'We still have many methods left. There's the chicken-walk, hanging from the wrists, the petrol finger . . .'

'The petrol finger?'

'Dip the finger in petrol and up the ass. It burns like hell. But we only use it in extreme cases.'

As he spoke, I suddenly became nervous that Santosh could hear me. And unnerved by the kind of revenge a man, especially a potentially innocent one, might later want to exact for listening in on men discussing the torments they still had in store for him, even as he endured some mild, late-afternoon torture, I hastened on.

The SHO's office was a dim room containing a large desk with a surface of brown glass. It was cluttered with softening grey files, coloured glass paperweights, bottles of diluter and Tipp-Ex and a yellow plastic pen holder. On one tube-lit wall, there hung a white board divided into columns of henious (*sic*) and non-henious (*sic*) crime. Just above kidnepping (*sic*) was house theft. The police claimed to have solved six of the fourteen crimes reported. Better odds, I must confess, than I had banked on.

'That six hopefully will become seven,' Vijay Singh said with a grin, as we sat down before him. He was also in plain clothes. His phone rang constantly; an elderly constable, standing by his desk, was appealing to him for more leave than he was due, wishing both to attend his father's memorial and his nephew's wedding. Vijay Singh was firmly telling him he couldn't take that much leave while trying to listen to Surinder Sharma brief him on the plan for investigating our robbery.

'Systematic, systematic,' he said, feigning interest in our case, 'everything should be systematic.' He gave orders for Santosh's house to be searched; he approved Surinder Sharma's plan to publish descriptions of the stolen goods in all the precinct's jewellery shops.

'Perhaps a description of the safe too,' Sharma suggested.

'Perhaps,' Vijay Singh confirmed. 'Was it a Godrej safe?'

'Yes,' I said.

'About this big?' he said, shaping its dimensions exactly with his hands.

'Yes,' I said.

He smiled at the impression he made, then closed in on a new phrase: 'But don't delay, don't delay. Must be no delay.'

It was at this point that Robin revealed what he had discovered about Dheeraj.

'Bring him in for remand immediately,' Vijay Singh said. 'What are you waiting for?'

'He's not here. He's on holiday.'

'When is he back?'

'Sunday,' I said. And having only just witnessed the departure of Dheeraj's sister, nephew and nieces twenty-four hours after their arrival in Delhi, I now advised that Dheeraj, newly married, twenty-two just the other day, and returning to Delhi after that same long journey from the hills, with his new bride in tow, be brought in for remand on arrival.

'We can do it the next day,' the policemen said, surprised at my urgency.

'No,' I replied coolly, 'I think we should do it that night itself. It's important that a surprise element work in our favour.'

Vijay Singh, with his special feeling for this manner of phrase, was impressed. 'Surprise element,' he repeated, relishing the sound of the words in his own mouth, 'surprise element. Yes, let's do it!'

A moment later his phone rang again, and becoming engaged in a lengthy conversation, he mouthed goodbye. When we left, the constable was still there, mournfully deciding between life and death.

Outside the police station a rural dusk was setting in. The small urban life of Chawalla was enveloped by immense and sudden night, carrying in its fall the smell of fields and returning cattle. The thunder and headlights of trucks down the thin stretch of road deepened the isolation. And once again it was possible to think of the road as river, but dark and solemn now, no longer a link, leaving Chawalla to its nowhereness.

We waited for a tube-lit chai/food/photostat shop to make a copy of Amit's Airtel record with its incriminating phone calls to our staff. A steady stream of out-of-uniform policemen went in and out. Surinder Sharma, feeling perhaps that he ought to treat me to a story from police life, began to tell me of the capture of the chain snatcher of Chawalla, beginning at the end.

'I'd received information about his whereabouts with great difficulty,' Sharma said, 'because he changed his location a lot. We arrived late at night at the building where he allegedly was. And very quietly we put police ladders against the walls and climbed up to the second-floor window. The first thing I see as I enter through the window is women sleeping. And I think, 'Shit, we're dead. We've been given the wrong information. Yet I continued, past the sleeping women, into the next room. And there they were, the men, asleep in chairs, absolutely talli. There was a table between them full of ashtrays and half-drunk bottles of liquor. On one side of the room was a mattress where the chain snatcher was passed out, a homemade gun under his pillow. Rehan saab, I'll say one thing about the man. The minute we nabbed him he confessed everything, and in such detail, that we knew it immediately to be the truth.'

'What did he say?'

'Only a few weeks before, he had been carrying out one of his operations when he began to suspect some of his confederates of cheating him. So he got the men together at one of his locations, and using the excuse of a party, began plying them with booze. He drank very little himself, waiting instead for them all to become talli before he questioned them. Though at first they denied the accusations, they were drunk and did not have their wits about them. Soon they began to make mistakes and the truth started coming out. The chain snatcher discovered they had cheated him out of nearly twenty thousand rupees, basically half the loot.

'When he heard this, he stabbed the men in several places, killing them on the spot. But he was not satisfied. Taking rocks, he smashed in their faces. He didn't want anyone to recognize them, you see. But still he was not satisfied. He had the bodies burnt to a cinder so that there would not be the smallest possibility of identifying them. But, Rehan saab, God is Great and when we finally found the remains of the bodies, in one of the pockets of the deceased we came upon an unburnt scrap of paper, on which a mobile phone number had been scrawled. It had gone out of use, but through the mobile phone company's records, we were able to trace it to the previous owner. That man turned out to be the uncle of one of the men who had been killed. When we tracked him down, he told us that his nephew had gone missing the month before. Then, by piecing together his movements – and it wasn't easy: the gang changed locations several times – we traced him to the chain snatcher.

'He was an amazing character, Rehan saab,' Sharma said with admiration, 'fearless and ingenious. Gold chains, you see, are very difficult to sell. But this guy hit upon a system, by which he would pawn the chains to a company, taking a loan in return. It's the kind of loan, which if you don't pay back in two years, the company gets ownership of the chain. This was what he did with each one. For years we had been getting reports of chain snatching incidents and they all originated from this one guy. We even arrested him once and broke up his group. But in court, a victim, who only days before had helped us identify the man, lost his nerve and said it wasn't him.'

'Why?'

'He'd received threats from the gang. He was a young man, at the beginning of his life; he didn't want to take a panga with such a big gangster. Can you believe, Rehan saab, that even in jail, this guy picked up time?'

'How?'

'He had taken a mobile phone into the jail with him. Naturally this is not allowed so when one of the other inmates saw him using it, he reported him to the warden. There and then, the man smashes the phone. But that night, he caught hold of the guy who had reported on him and,' Sharma explained, his eyes widening, 'screwed him. He had unnatural sex with him. What did he care? We could book him under 377, the unnatural sex act, but we couldn't hang him twice.'

Surinder Sharma had a strange admiration for the criminals he had known. It was as if he saw himself as a small sad impediment in their depraved, but for at least a while, pleasure-filled existence. And almost like someone confessing to having wasted his life ruining the fun of others, he reported that he had been passed over for promotion for the tenth year running. 'Even the position I would have been promoted to was no big deal. I would have had it for a while, then it would have been time to retire me.'

'What about the sleeping girls?' I asked abruptly, hoping to change the doleful direction the conversation was taking.

'Keep girls,' he replied, and again with relish: 'keep girls for screwing purposes.'

At that precise moment there was some commotion near the gates of the station. An elderly woman dressed in an off-white kurta and a red dupatta appeared out of a police vehicle. A lock of silver hair had fallen over her lined and distressed face.

'She's to be arrested,' Surinder Sharma said and chuckled.

'Why?'

'She's been accused by her daughter-in-law of violence and harassment. Then a few days ago the girl drank poison.'

'Did she die?'

'No, no, that's the funny thing. It's a false case. The daughter-in-law is the one who has been harassing her mother-in-law, forcing her to put their family plot in her name. Her husband, you see, is an alcoholic and does nothing all day. When the mother-in-law refused, the girl drank poison. But she didn't drink very much. She drank just enough to be hospitalized. She was discharged the next day. We had to go because it was a poisoning case, but we knew instantly that it was false.'

'How did you know it was false?'

'The girl refused to put blame on anyone except her mother-in-law. When we questioned her, saying that it was strange that no one else should have participated in the harassment, the answer she gave was that her father-in-law was a heart patient and her sister-in-law an asthma patient.'

'How should that make any difference?' I asked in complete confusion.

'Exactly!' Surinder Sharma said, now laughing. 'That's the point. She was afraid that if they were arrested and something happened to them, then she was in for it. So she chose her mother-in-law to blame.'

'But then why is the mother-in-law being arrested?'

'Procedure, Rehan saab, procedure.'

Robin, who had been standing over the photocopying machine, taking an inexplicably long time, drifted over.

'Everything ready?' Surinder Sharma asked.

'Everything set.'

'Then drop saab home and I'll meet you back here in ten minutes or so?'

'Drop me home? Why? What's happening?'

Robin, his face hardly visible in the dark, whispered, 'We're going to search Santosh's house.'

'Would you like to come?' Surinder Sharma said recklessly.

'No, no, absolutely not,' Robin answered for me.

'Why?' I asked, though I already knew the answer.

'You know, even if there's one per cent risk you should not be there.'

'Risk of what?'

'Bas, "the police is harassing us," a riot-shiot breaks out . . .'

I agreed and we said goodbye to Surinder Sharma, who was going inside to change into his uniform.

On the way to the car, I casually asked Robin why the same reasons for not going didn't apply to him. Though it was not said, I think the idea was that my privilege and English-speaking background would single me out for some special brand of resentment. But now Robin wondered if he was not so unprivileged himself. And though not a fickle man, he suddenly changed his mind. Not just this; he asked if I would go back into the police station and tell Surinder Sharma that I had forbidden him from going. What strange and unprofessed fears we were all living with!

I did as Robin asked; went back inside and excused him from having to go. Surinder Sharma, now in olive-green trousers and a white vest, smiled knowingly.

That night Sharma and Vijay Singh paid us a final visit in Steeple Hall. Dheeraj had arrived a few hours before, suntanned and freckled from the hills. My mother had called him in, assuring him that though her suspicions rested on his brother-in-law, he would be spared if he confessed.

'I know you know who did it,' she said.

A smile appeared on his round handsome face. It could at once have been a smile of utter incredulity or mal-evolence.

'I wasn't even here . . .'

'Don't try that with me, Dheeraj. I know that the safe was taken well before you left for holiday. And what were you doing calling . . .'

'Ah, ah, ah, Ma. Stop it,' I said in English. 'Remember the surprise element.'

We both thought we saw him pale.

'I can't stop the investigation,' my mother said threat-eningly, 'but if you come clean, I promise you there will be no danger.'

Leaving the room, he said that he more than anyone wanted to make sure the thief was caught. But this of course was not enough.

Then security experts, a retired colonel and a silent Sikh gentleman, arrived. They brought with them three bouncers in dark-blue shirts and trousers, plus three armed guards. They filled my mother with new fears and futilities.

'Your security was definitely in on it, madam. Other-wise, it is inconceivable that they should not have made their rounds on the night of the theft.' Then breaking off, they said the worst thing of all: 'The problem is that, now that the police know the size of the heist, even if they catch the guys, it will only be so that they can get the loot for themselves and they'll give the thieves a cut to keep them quiet.'

This last bit of information brought home the full reality of the charade the investigation had been: a rite of mutual degradation, where evil – as with the Sanskrit word for it – was one with futility.

'But rest assured,' the security experts continued, 'I have brought, for your peace of mind, three guards and three bouncers who will take rounds all night till this thing is resolved. No one will enter or leave the premises without their permission. I should say, however, that the bouncers are extraneous. They are there only for your peace of mind. Because though they look fearsome, they are unarmed and can stand no chance against armed robbers.'

Soon after they had gone, Vijay Singh and Sharma arrived. My mother called them into the drawing room and they came in diffidently. I could see she was trying to sweeten them into doing something about the robbery, telling them that she was a lawyer and wanted to know about their lives.

'Our lives,' Vijay Singh said, 'are miserable. Ask Sharma. I haven't been home to see my wife for three days. We work fourteen hours without a break. I'm not saying I don't want to work, but it should be proportionate.'

'It's a terrible job,' Sharma affirmed, 'the hours are terrible. We feel so stretched.'

Having struck upon a word he liked, Vijay Singh said again, 'Proportionate. It needs to be proportionate.'

For some moments they spoke of police reform, then gently, my mother steered the conversation toward the case.

'Ninety-nine per cent inside job, ma'am.'

My mother looked grave.

'But let's see,' Sharma said, 'we'll haul in a few people. That fellow Santosh is still with us. Tonight you're sending someone else across.'

'Yes, Dheeraj,' I said.

'Good. Perhaps something will come out. I see that you have new security.'

'Yes,' I said, following my mother's lead, 'times are such that we now have security to watch our security.'

The men laughed. And then to my great surprise Vijay Singh asked my mother, as if this were a Sunday night ritual between them, if she might lend him something to read.

'Happily,' she said, feeling perhaps this would help our cause, 'Hindi or English?'

'English,' the policeman replied.

'Fiction or non-fiction?'

'Something about history or politics perhaps.'

My mother rose and returned a few minutes later with a copy of *An Area of Darkness*.

Before leaving, Sharma, clearly still thinking of our earlier conversation, said, 'Yes, a terrible job. Everyone comes out tainted.'

The next day Santosh had been too badly beaten to come to work. Dheeraj, with only one bad night behind him, came in though, his suntanned face red and washed with tears. He had no idea who took this safe. The police had slapped him and abused him and kept him there all night. Please; he wanted to be spared, he had nothing to do with all this business. You can ask Kalyan; I came back last night and had a fight with him; I said if you know anything please tell madam. I can't go in there again.'

'Then what were you doing speaking to Amit for fifteen minutes?' I intervened.

'There was a problem with the Internet. You told me

to get it fixed. I knew he knew how to fix it so I called him.'

'For fifteen minutes you spoke about the Internet?'

'No,' he said and suddenly became sheepish. 'There was something else.'

'What?' my mother and I said in one voice.

'He'd just been for a pilgrimage to Vaishnodevi and I wanted to know what it was like. We spoke about that.'

I felt what last strength I had drain from me. I couldn't take any more of these details, alongside these casual brutalities. I saw my mother's face fill with grief. As a last hope that he might be lying, I glanced quickly at the copy of the Airtel statement. In the column listing the service provider, it said next to the fifteen minute call, Airtel–J&K. Jammu and Kashmir, the state where Vaishnodevi was.

And seeing him now in this condition, we were like people who, speaking a foreign language, are surprised to find the words having their effect on people to whom they are not foreign. Had our permitting the police to thrash him really resulted in him being thrashed? There would be no more, my mother assured him. Let them do what they like, but Dheeraj would not be beaten any more. We were sure of his innocence. Kalyan, on the other hand, was seeming guiltier than ever.

And yet, neither my mother nor I was able to remain in the house while the thrashings continued. We left Steeple Hall together the following day. She went back to Calcutta and I to the Sethia company bungalow in town.

Before leaving, Kalyan approached me to say that he wanted to speak to me about something, but preferred to do it in town. He came a few days later. With Dheeraj's beating curtailed, the police had come full circle to him. He had his second appointment with them that night.

He was, as he had been on that first morning, when he reported the robbery, his eyes clear and black, as if kohled, his long-nailed hands hanging by his side. He had no definite idea who had done it, but he had recently developed some suspicions. Did I know that Narender, the electrician, was in a legal case in his village? And he had had to shell out some four or five lakhs in damages? Now where would someone like him get that kind of money? Coming home after his thrashing the night before, Kalyan said someone had driven past him on a bike/scooter, and slapping him on the back of the head, said, 'Blab and you're dead.'

Poor Kalyan, I thought. There were no depths to his stupidity after all; he was simply stupid. And at the end of this ten-day trauma, he had learnt very crudely to lie.

The information about Narender was old and known to everyone. He told me one story about the threat made to him and another to the police. This was all the deceit that had forced its way out of him after his ordeal. This was the best he could do as far as survival instincts went. I dismissed him and turned my gaze back to the television where – of far greater interest to me than Kalyan's pathetic story – the London bombers' friends and relations were being interviewed. It was the last time I saw him.

* * *

I had sought isolation, but found myself more isolated than I knew. And this was not the innocence of my childhood. Though no less blinding, these isolations were of an India whose worst nature was hidden from herself. A protective screen of encoded privilege – not simply as money, but as aspects of privilege, English, Western dress, values and manners: the things that put me above caste in India – made injustice, and especially cruelty, of the most casual variety, appear always as the work of others. It was, and by extension, its taint, something that just went on in the society, but for which its educated classes bore no responsibility. And with this sphere of deep remove in place, and the question of agency diverted, one could almost be allowed to feel that there was no cost to living around this daily violence.

But there was one thing, one poison, in some ways the supreme evil, that was able to seep past these protections, setting slowly to its work of corroding the moral interior. Complicity. Complicity, with its supporting cast of shallowness, indifference, apathy and inaction, was, in a sense, the most untraceable of the great evils. And yet like the salinity, invisible and caustic, that travels in brackish water, it would bring its white and brittle decay to all those natures it came into contact with, decimating in them for ever the hope of finer feeling.

I, with my palate still sensitive, found its taste new and strong, but my response, arising out of habit, was weak and familiar. I cut short my summer in Delhi and called in the advantage of one further degree of removal, the one that would always stand in the way of myself and the Indian reality: the advantage of retreat, of being able to leave.

And already, in the Zurich duty-free a few days later, a night flight behind me, a boarding pass to Boston in my pocket, Delhi felt far away, that hard hot land impossible to imagine. In the new cooler place that awaited me, of air-conditioned bookshops and iced-coffees, of summer schools and internships, I would remake myself, I would find an intellectual stent to channel out the bad memory of Steeple Hall. My sensitivities would return, the soul would purify and become once again presentable to Zack and my professors in Massachusetts.

And that is how it was. I returned the next winter to Delhi, a year after a devastating earthquake in the Kashmir valley, and weeks after I had met the Tabassums for the first time. The heat was gone; the air was cool and smoky; and, erasing all trace of what had gone on there, were the new staff at Steeple Hall.

4

Port bin Qasim: An Idyll

(2011)

جو بھی ہے پروردۂ شب، جو بھی ہے ظلمت پرست

وہ تو جائیں گے اسی جانب، جدھر جائے گی رات

ہے اُفق پر ایک سنگِ آفتاب آنے کی دیر

ٹوٹ کر مانندِ آئینہ، بکھر جائے گی رات

Suroor Barabankvi

A syntactically unfaithful translation: There is upon the horizon the
anticipation of a stone-like sun/ As a mirror shattering, the night will
scatter/ All those who worship darkness, those who have been reared on
twilight/ they must go as goes the night.

The Tabassums! Sahil Tabassum, you know, once said to me, years after I had met him, 'I like a book to have a beginning, a middle and an end.' I thought to myself, answering cliché with cliché, if everyone has a book in them, mine cannot be that kind of book. The gaps in my life were too many, the threads too few. And though I knew this, knew there was little to string life together, the tendency was still to appear as whole before the world, to let the imagination fill in the spaces that experience had left blank.

A mistake, I now feel.

In writing this last episode, I tried often to see what I had not seen, to be places I had not been, to pretend that my view of Port bin Qasim had not only – and ever – been an eclipsed one. In this, I was like a man, who peeping through a keyhole, is denied his vantage point, when leaning too forcefully against the door that has restricted (and excited) his vision, he causes it to swing wide open. A mistake, you see: for what we cannot know is as much a part of us as what we do know. And people, like places, must learn to live with their absences, with those parts of the record that have been sanitized.

This story came to me during – and I think you will see why – a final visit to my father's country. I was tempted many times to abandon it, for the material is strange and distressing, and the tale without moral, unless you consider looking and recording with a sympathetic eye as moral enough. But, in the end, the writing need was too strong; and, for all my misgivings, it made its way onto the page.

One morning in May, when the sun was already high over the tarmac, I stepped off the plane in Port bin Qasim for the first time. Even deep inland, where the airport stood, surrounded by pale hard land, there was the briny breath of the sea. Overhead, casting the ominous shapes of birds of prey, were the frayed crowns of palm trees. There was in this play of short shadows and flickering wind-blown sunlight a noontime menace. And about the young man, who appeared from a line of unfamiliar faces, with a piece of board that bore the name 'Rehan Tabassum' there was the scent of guns, dollars and drugs.

He knew me immediately. His tall, slim figure pushed its way out of the crowd; he was smiling knowingly at me.

'My God, saab,' he said, extending a sunburned hand. 'You are Mr Sahil exact. Even more than your brothers, you look like him. And Mr Narses gave me this . . .' He waved aside the name card, now folded in half. Some strands of his long hair blew across his face; his eyes were very black; his lips had a chiselled prominence that made them ideal for the expression of amusement; and, I suppose, though there was not a trace of it now, cruelty.

He was wounded by my initial lack of recognition.

'You don't know who I am?' he said, adding loudly, 'Mirwaiz! From the train in Kashmir? The year after the earthquake? The lake? Don't you remember?'

'Mirwaiz, my God! I don't believe it. What are you doing here?'

'Bas,' he said, smiling sheepishly now. 'I drifted around, started looking for work. I applied at Qasimic Call for the job of a peon, and as I was waiting in the corridor, who should walk by but your brother, Mr Isffy. I stopped him there and then and told him who I was, and, I hope you don't mind, used your name too. I said you were my friend, and when Mr Isffy heard my story, he said he had already heard it once before from you. So, at least, back then you remembered, Rehan saab! Bas, that was what did it; when he put two and two together, he gave me a job on the spot. I worked with him a while, and later he arranged for me to be transferred to Mr Narses's private residence. That's where I am now.'

All I could do was congratulate him. And he, as if feeling we had shared beginnings, congratulated me in turn.

'What for?'

'For your re-entry into the family, of course.'

Then glancing at his watch, he said abruptly, 'Come on. Mr Narses will be waiting. The car is just here.'

He pointed at a dark green SUV and was about to turn on his heels, when he remembered my bags. He returned to lift them with the extreme graciousness of a man deigning to do work below his station. It drew my attention to other things about him – his impeccable toilette, his good looks, his fashionable clothes, the brushed and shampooed hair. And, for a moment, I had a suspicion about whether Mirwaiz was really a servant. There had always been a lot of strange talk about my father's brother-in-law, Narses ul-Hijr – a short, and, by all accounts, unconsummated marriage; no woman since; obesity in later life; and an unhealthy obsession with the

Tabassum men, especially my father, and their love lives. I wondered if Mirwaiz was not the most recent chapter in a familiar tale.

He, for his part, was still full of seductions. On the drive into town, within moments of my saying that it was my intention to stay some weeks in Port bin Qasim, then travel gradually by road to La Mirage, he offered to drive me. 'I'll take you,' he said, laughing jauntily, 'Narses saab, and I have been many times. The roads are beautiful now. We'll stop in little-known towns. You'll see desert first, then fertile fields in Punjab. There are famous shrines along the way, and all the country's rivers. The Indus, the Sutlej, the Jhelum . . .'

'Have you been working for Narses long?' I asked.

'No, well, yes. Off and on,' he said, and smiled. 'I ran away in the middle, but then came back.'

'Where did you go?'

'Dubai,' he said, looking quickly over at me.

'You really get around! What happened?' I asked. 'Why did you leave?'

'This happened,' he answered, and turning his face from the road, caused a smooth and vicious scar to uncoil and stretch itself out across his neck.

'How did you get that?'

'Football. Knife,' Mirwaiz muttered.

'And that was why you left Dubai?' I asked, forming a new sense of his restlessness.

'Yes. Why else?' Mirwaiz replied. 'It's the people that make a place. And if the people do this to you,' he added, trailing a finger down the scar, 'you have to move on.'

Not a servant, for sure, I thought to myself, and vain too. He had evidently seen a lot in the five years since we last met, and the exposure had sharpened his instincts, made him more a man of the world. He was strangely of a piece with the mood of this new city, with the hint of threat that seemed contained in its pale cloudless sky and the distant presence of sea.

Traffic lights flew past us, palms lay felled over the highways, which merged fast with new highways. Eventually the traffic slowed and the city approached. Its appearance made real my arrival in Port bin Qasim, forcing me to consider why I was really here.

There was Sahil Tabassum, of course, my father, the man of small beginnings, who had lived many lives, and made good in each one. He had been a finance man in Dubai in the days he had known my mother; after their relationship was over, he had returned to La Mirage to be a politician, fighting General Gul's military tyranny;

when that ended, he spent some years in and out of power; then, with the return of military rule, he became a businessman, building a news and telecom empire out of nothing. That was what he had been, a media tycoon of a kind, a man of dark suits and sunglasses, when I first met him in La Mirage five years before. He had married again and had three other children with Shaista, a young wife twenty years his junior. Though there was much that was interesting about him, I found him a difficult man to reach. It was as if the many lives he had lived had made him intolerant of the past. And I, who sought him out from the deepest folds of his past, was not someone he could easily communicate with.

We had blood and almost nothing else in common.

But blood was something and, in those first few years, we tried to make a go of our unlikely bond. Our relationship progressed haltingly and was marked by a kind of stage fright in each other's presence, as though we were both aware that if we had met under different circumstances, we might have seen better men. Our uneasiness made us, each in our own way, create proxies, people and conditions through which and under which we could be both together and apart. His were his wife and daughters; mine were my brothers. Through these people we felt our relationship deepen, felt indeed its warmth, without ever having to face its discomfort. And though he wasn't here, Port bin Qasim now was one such situation, a way to be both near and aloof. My true reason, though, for being in the city was not my father at all but older brother, Isphandiyar Tabassum.

I had missed out on Isffy when I first met the other Tabassums. He had still been in the cold then and I was told specifically not to contact him. At the time, the reason for his banishment was kept from me. My siblings said that he and our father didn't really get along; that was all. But one night in La Mirage, my eldest sister, born of my father's first marriage, spoke to me about the real truth, and once she had, it was not hard to see why it had been withheld.

My brother had slept with, then lived with, and then threatened to marry, an old girlfriend of my father's. I say girlfriend, but she was really just someone my father had slept with on more than one occasion. What made the whole affair the more distasteful to the Tabassums, and especially to my father, was that the girl was nearly ten years older than Isffy, and of damaged reputation. Sahil Tabassum had said when he heard: 'Why does he have to bring home the girl the rest of the world just fucks?'

His reaction was, I learned from my sister, characteristic. For, apparently, he had always interfered in Isffy's love life, and my sister spoke almost fearfully of Isffy's motivations for dating our father's ex. 'What Abba can't escape,' she had said, 'is not that the girl was ten years older, of bad reputation, and an ex-flame of his, but that it was *because* she was all of these things that Isffy loved her. Abba knew it was his way of taking revenge.'

'Revenge for what?'

'For all the times in the past that Isffy had been trifled with, when Narses and Abba would get in the way of him and his girlfriends. I remember one summer he had brought home a girl from the LSE. She was Moldavian, I think; Nadia was her name. A very nice girl, pretty, and bright too. But Abba, from the moment he saw her, wouldn't address two words to her. If he passed her in the corridor, on the way to the pool, his eyes would run cold. Behind her back, and encouraging the little ones to join in too, they — Shaista, Abba, Narses — would make fun of her, referring to her as "Isffy's Bosnian refugee". It was terrible. The girl, feeling unwelcome, began to lose her nerve, and having been perfectly relaxed and plucky when she arrived, became sulky and needy. Isffy, who had been so in love with her in the beginning, began to doubt his judgement. Worse still, Narses, with Abba's approval, made it seem that the girl was a bad influence on Isffy, disrupting his studies and generally holding him back. And Isffy, because he was still young then, believed them. I can't tell you: it didn't happen once; it happened ten times! Those first break-ups were made like offerings to Abba, who accepted them with love and blessings. But as Isffy got older,' my sister had said, 'he grew wise to what they were up to and the break-ups became harder to extract, often needing threats and ultimatums, all, invariably, presented by Narses.'

That last time, when Isffy had been too much in the cold for me to be allowed to meet him, they had reached their deepest impasse. Isffy had found a girl who was truly inappropriate and the break-up was impossible to obtain. Isffy had left home over it, spending nearly two years away, living under the illusion that his indignation alone would deliver him independence. He had vilified our father to all who were willing to listen; he was apparently a regular act at the Gymkhana Club bar. But the financial brokerage he tried setting up with a friend, and on to which his hopes of independence were pinned, sank fast. Those last few months of debt and danger were so severe that even our father, not one to shorten the time those who defied him stewed, was forced to act fast and bail Isffy out. No sooner had he done it – before he had – than there were new terms. On the one hand, the car, the house, the job to remind Isffy what coming home felt like, on the other the clean ultimatum: never see the girl again.

I had met Isffy for the first time in La Mirage, the year he accepted the new terms. I remember him having a weary and sensitive face, with still something defiant about it. Surrounded by the other Tabassums, some his full sisters, others the children of my father's younger wife, all more malleable than him, all happy under the tyranny of our father, I sensed him holding back. He sipped his whisky quietly in the corner; he joked and laughed, but he was uneasy. It was as if he also knew a shade of my experience, of feeling diminished in our father's presence. Because of our shared trouble with our father and because I knew him the least, Isffy, of all my father's family, had the largest claim on my imagination. The chance now to see him at his ease, in his own environment as it were, was one of the main reasons I was looking forward to my time in Port bin Qasim.

Mirwaiz opened a button of his bright printed shirt, and blew down his chest.

'Hot, no?' he said. 'It's just started, the heat. I can't take it even slightly, you know?'

We entered a commercial area. The road was lined

with shops and restaurants whose blue and green glass frontage reflected with vacant intensity the treeless stretch.

'Where are we going?' I asked.

'Aylanto,' Mirwaiz said easily. 'Have you been there before?'

'No. It's my first time in the city.'

'You'll love it. It's new. Mr Narses says that,' and now he spoke in English, 'the calamari fritti is out of this world.' He turned to me and grinned.

'Have you tried it?' I asked with astonishment.

'No,' Mirwaiz said, 'I don't eat seafood. I prefer a place in Defence called . . .'

He was still speaking when, looking up, I saw in the distance, where I had expected to see the glitter of water, a human sea of black and green. Against the haze of the day, it seemed to flicker and fade, like the black spots that appear before one's eyes from direct contact with the sun. Carrying over it was a dull and distant roar.

'What is that?' I asked.

'I don't know,' Mirwaiz replied, seeming to want to shield me from it, 'a protest of some sort. I'll find out. This country is crazy, you know, Rehan saab. But don't worry. I'll wait with you till someone arrives. Look, here's Aylanto.'

It stood on one corner of the shopping street and had, as part of its Spanish colonial theme, a pale yellow facade with crooked rustication and green louvred windows. A group of valets, thin anxious men with glazed eyes and untidy stubble, lingered outside. They were dressed, despite the great heat, in black trousers, limp black waistcoats and grimy shirts, their bow ties wilting in the sun.

'Do you know what's going on?' Mirwaiz asked one of them, stepping out of the car and handing him the keys.

'It seems, sir,' the man said hurriedly, 'that there is a protest on.'

'I can see that, too, genius. What's it against?'

'English,' the man replied, with some confusion.

Mirwaiz gave a derisive chuckle.

'You see, Rehan saab, how mad the people in this country are? Everything is abstraction. You watch, there'll be a protest against oxygen next.'

At the glass-fronted shoe shops and boutiques, with their bright signage and billboards, all in English, the protestors rose to frenzy. Like the tail of some reptilian creature, they moved fast down the street. Where their vandalism opened up bare cement spaces over the shopfronts, they spray-painted sprawling slogans in black.

Mirwaiz read the painted letters on their green satin banners. 'Jago!' he muttered. 'Awake. Fools: if they had any idea that that was a Sanskrit word, they would grow madder still. Chalo, saab, you'd better go inside.'

A silver Honda screeched out of a side street, its bonnet and windscreen ablaze.

'Mr Isphandiyar's car,' Mirwaiz whispered. Then suddenly intimate, he said: 'Rehan saab, how well do you actually know these people, the Tabassums . . . ?'

'Not very well at all,' I replied.

'Then just remember this,' Mirwaiz said with new urgency, 'your father, Mr Tabassum, is the law. He is the sun in this strange universe. Everyone else exists, be it good or bad, by his light. Don't bother looking for an external logic,' he continued, gesturing inexplicably at the crowd. 'There is none. Everything,' he said, pointing at the closed interior of the restaurant, 'is to be found within. Mr Isffy, he's a good guy. He has issues, sure; and our relationship is not what it used to be; but he'll be your number one ally, believe me.'

Seeing Isffy emerge from his car, Mirwaiz said hastily: 'Chal, darling, I'll hand you over to him and take off. Phir milenge. Soon. And speak to Narses saab about the trip north. Tell him you want to take Mirwaiz travelling,'

he effused, as if conjuring up a medieval idea of wander,
'and I'm yours.'

I had turned to leave when I heard him say, 'Rehan
saab, what's your number?'

'I don't have one.'

'How can that be? Sahil Tabassum's son and no
number? Here take this.' He reached into the glovebox
of the car and took out a plastic CD case containing a
yellow and green booklet, with a pay-as-you-go card. 'It's
a Qasimic Call card. Your natural right, as the owner's
son. Put the sim into your phone and I'll maro you a
missed call this evening.'

A few moments later, we sat in the cool of the restaurant,
sipping two green non-alcoholic cocktails. Lunching ladies
with glossy lips in two shades of brown picked at large
salads.

'You should have seen what I saw,' my brother said,
speaking of the demonstration, 'the rage was surreal. I
witnessed this one scene in a jewellery shop belonging to
an old man. Some hoodlums had barged in and started
doing todh-phodh, tearing down all the things in his shop
that were written in English. The old man didn't say a
word. He sat back and let them do what they wanted.

But when they were done, he called over one of the boys and said in a very calm voice, "Could you tell me the time?" The boy was obviously a bit startled by his reaction. Anyway, he did as he was asked. And just as the guy turns his hand over to look at his watch, you know what this old man does? He tears the watch from his wrist, throws it on the floor and starts stamping on it till he's smashed its face. All the while, he's screaming, spit flying from his mouth, "English! English! English! Even your Time is in English. You've destroyed my shop for nothing; you'll never be free of English."'

I half-listened to my brother. I felt a deep sense of contentment at being in his presence. It was like the comfort of being a child in Delhi when, out with my mother at night, I would fall asleep on somebody's sofa to the sound of adult voices.

There was something unreal and marvellous for me about having an elder brother. I had sought this bond with male friends in the past, but it had always felt laboured. Here it was built into the relationship, a part of its nature, and could even, it seemed – this being the greatest relief of all – be taken for granted.

'And do you know what the cause of it is?' Isffy said, focusing my attention.

'What?' I asked, aware that our political conversation

now was a Tabassum tactic – our father's really – of overcoming the awkwardness after a long separation.

'That same vision of purity on which the country was founded. The feeling that if only we were purer we would be better.'

'More Islam?'

'Yes and no. What people coming from outside don't realize is that the rot is secular; it has no religion. The place is full of gangs, kidnappings, parricides, rapes, murders, you name it. So when someone says Islamic revolution, it brings to mind something terribly organized. But nothing as organized as that can come out of this chaos. Islam hides the real picture; it has always done that here. Where are you staying, by the way?' he said, abruptly.

'I don't know. Narses suggested I stay at the Qasimic Call guest house . . .'

'Forget it!' Isffy said. 'You're staying with me. It's not every day that my long-lost brother comes to town.'

Then I remembered my bags and Mirwaiz. But my brother had anticipated me. 'I've already told the court eunuch's butt boy,' he said, 'to put your bags in my car.'

The aggression with which he spoke allowed me to speak more intimately.

'I hope they're not giving you a rough time?' I said.

'No,' he replied, and feigning, I felt, indifference, added, 'they're always trying, of course. But at the moment I'm handling the family's TV channel, which is doing well and pulling in tons of advertising. That makes them happy. Plus, I'm producing a news show called *The Fifth Column*, which has very high TRPs. So things are on an even keel for now. But that doesn't mean I'd let my guard down. And now that I'm back in the family, I want to fix that hijra, Narses, once and for all.'

'Isffy, be careful.'

'Just wait and see. He's also vulnerable. Now I'll show him how it feels.'

'Vulnerable? Why?'

'Because,' Isffy said, holding my gaze over the bubble glass rim of the lime passion, 'he's in love, for the first time, with a man other than my father.'

'Mirwaiz?'

'Ye-ess.'

'Isffy, how horrible! He's hardly older than I am. How did he end up there, anyway? I thought it was you who hired him?'

'I did. For the office. But Narses took one look at him and snatched him up. Are you shocked? Why? Abba's no different. When he married Shaista, she was my age.'

'I suppose.' Then I recalled how my father would

often say to my youngest brother, light-eyed and handsome, 'I don't care if you're a rapist, a murderer, a serial
killer, if you're a gay I'll kill you.' Were he to find out
about Mirwaiz, I thought to myself, Narses's little secret,
perhaps the first he had ever had from our father, was
sure to end in tragedy.

'Is he so bad, Narses?' I asked.

My brother sighed: 'No, of course, not. No one is all
bad. But he's played a very destructive role in our family.
His willingness to live by the light of my . . . our father
has made it the norm for everyone else. He was like the
second man to nod and say, "Yes, the world is flat." After
that, the third, fourth, fifth were easy to find.' Then, as
though wishing to give me some hard evidence, he said,
'You know, he's got me under constant watch at Qasimic
Call, looking for anything he can hold against me, report-
ing every last slip-up to my father. You can, I suppose,
blame Abba for allowing this to happen, but it's as if
Narses feeds his worst instincts. Which are to control and
dominate the people near him, as if they were one of his
small businesses.'

Presently a flash of sunlight went through the restaurant. The gloom resettled, but the new arrival delayed
his entry. He lingered in an anteroom of sorts, talking
on the phone, his figure partially concealed by a pair of

louvred batwing doors. All that was visible was the hem of his cream kurta and a pair of black Peshawari sandals. He had his back to the restaurant, but in the heaviness of the neck, the thickness of his fingers and the strain in the raised elbow, his great bulk was apparent.

He spoke loudly; he made self-deprecating jokes – 'But mian saab it was *because* they put me in the back of the plane that it could land at all' – he alternated between addressing his interlocutor as mian saab, chief and boss. From the adoration in his voice, the repeated jokes, the booming laughter it was clear to the entire restaurant whom he was speaking to.

'Abba,' Narses wetly mouthed to us as he swung around, resting two heavy arms on the flimsy doors, causing their hinges to whine. His face, almost as if the fat had acted as a preservative, was youthful. He had a full head of hair, a middle-parting, pinkish cheeks, full lips, and – as with many fat people – put forward the illusion that if only he were thin he would be good-looking.

Having alerted both father and sons of each other's presence, he played on our discomfort, knowing that neither of us would cramp our style enough to ask to speak to the other or even to send a friendly word of greeting. Yet, when the conversation was over, we would all three be left with some resentment that the other had not asked after him.

'Mian saab, you are too much!' Narses suddenly exclaimed, bellowing into the darkened room; the lunching ladies and restaurant staff tittered as if they too had been included in the joke. 'Now you've really shown me. I must tell Isffy and Rehan. Yes, they're sitting here, looking as if they were joined at birth. They are sure to roar with laughter. OK, chief, now before you ring off without a word, I'm going to say bye first. Bye now. Bye. Bye.'

Then looking at the phone with dismay, Narses ul-Hijr, with the ease of a man accustomed to making dramatic entries, addressed the whole room: 'He's done it again. Twenty-five years now he's been my brother-in-law and not once has he ever said hello or bye to me. I know the conversation's over when there's no one on the other end. In any event, Mir Anwar,' Narses added, looking towards the restaurant manager who now rushed up to him, 'he sends his warmest regards to you and your family. He never forgets the kindness people showed him during those dark days of the 1980s when we thought Gul's tyranny would never end.'

The manager beamed. 'Thank you, Mr Narses, sir. Please also convey my warmest regards to Mr Sahil. He is a valiant hero of this country. I will never forget his courage.'

'Good, good, Meeru. Now, tell me: broadband working fine?'

The manager nodded. 'Sir with your duas. Thank you. I am, you know, a loyal Qasimic Call customer.'

'I know, Meeru. And QC is what it is because of the duas of people like you.'

'Yes, Mr Narses, sir. How many companies now?'

'Eleven,' Narses replied with such amazement that it was as though he had himself posed the question. 'Can you believe it? From one room in Mr Tabassum's house to a conglomerate of eleven companies. At the time he'd just left politics. I was handling his finances so I can tell you he didn't have fifty thousand rupees to his name. Can you believe it, a man of fifty with no more than fifty thousand roops in his bank account. And six children to support.'

I had been left out of the count. Narses looked over to us and bunched up his fingers so as to give the impression that the conversation took place out of our earshot. Isffy looked at me with fatigue, as though he had seen these sycophantic performances many times before. Narses, having turned back to the manager, was saying: 'But he had foresight. He saw then, now fifteen years ago, that the future was communication. He began small: with phone cards and cyber-optic cables, then broadband, cable network, payphones, LDI, wireless. He branched out: he dammed one revenue stream and channelled it into another area. He worked on margins, he scaled economies. He didn't waste a breath. When he wasn't working, he was reading. His first love was politics remember, not business. So he had to learn it all from scratch. He tells me, "Narses, when I began I didn't know that equity had nothing to do with horses and liquidity, nothing to do with water."'

'Sir, good one!' Meeru laughed. 'Must remember that. Good one, sir, good one.'

Narses, seeing the components of his joke fall into place, laughed too. His very white, unusually long teeth showed. He seemed more boyish than ever. There was something of the tragedy of late Elvis about him, of the weight having come to the still youthful face.

Serious again, he went on: 'But now look at the result: he has channels, a newspaper, shopping malls here and in La Mirage, real estate, a brokerage house. And you know he oversees every company himself. I handle the broker-age side of things. So if you don't mind my saying it . . .'

'No, sir, please, anything . . .' the manager said.

'Liquidity! I can't pass solidity without the man finding

out. I have so much as to open my nada and he calls: "Narses, what the bloody hell do you think you're up to?" My little nephew, Saif,' he said, now once again looking over to us and bunching up his fingers into a petitioning flower, 'has opened a bowling alley and go-cart company. A small thing, you know, a children's thing. But mind you, a money-earner. The boy's sharp like his dad. Do you know, a day doesn't go by when Mr Tabassum is not himself aware of how many carts have gone around those tracks, how many balls have rolled down those alleys.'

The manager held so far in thrall became confidential. He took Narses aside and they spoke for a few minutes, now truly out of earshot. When they were finished, Narses nodded. 'I'll look into it, Meeru. I'll see what I can do. Tell the boy to come and see me.'

'Will do, sir.'

Then, maintaining a furtive expression of concern, Narses surveyed the restaurant. Seeing no familiar diners, his eye paused gravely on our empty glasses.

'Meeru, get the boys another drink, will you?'

'Sir, of course. Another lime passion?'

'Lime passion? I like it. Get me one too. But none . . .' Narses made a gesture of a bottle pouring, 'of *that* passion for me.'

'No, sir,' the manager replied, 'all our drinks are non-alcoholic.'

When he had taken leave of Narses, the manager came up to Isffy and shook his hand warmly. 'It's such a pleasure to have you dining with us again, son. I've known you since you were this high,' he said putting his hand to his waist. 'At the time Mr Tabassum was in and out of Faisalabad Jail. The Gul years, you know. He was so brave, I can't tell you, son. Once, I remember, they had him in a cage for thirty-six hours. In the day they would cover it in a black leather cloth and sprinkle water on it to raise the humidity inside. They wanted him to sign an admission of treason. We had all signed, but not your father. They couldn't get him to crack. When he came back to the cell after being tortured for days, we asked him how he had withstood it. And do you know what he said: "It was nothing, Meeru. They made a miscalculation; that was all. They dragged it on too long. If they had asked in the first twelve hours, I would have signed anything. But when a man exceeds what he thought were his limits, he becomes a little cocky." Very brave, a tiger of Punjab.'

The manager's praise of our father seemed to make Isffy uncomfortable, and he was visibly relieved when

Meeru asked, with a quick look in my direction, 'Your friend?'

'No, my brother!' Isffy exclaimed. 'Can you believe it?'

Doubt entered Mir Anwar's face. He seemed to be trying to work out how this was possible. At last smiling from embarrassment, he said, 'Saif . . .'

'No, no, Rehan,' Issfy replied, taking a strange pleasure in the awkwardness of the situation. 'A brother from *yet* another mother.'

Mir Anwar must have felt it was not right to ask more. But welcoming me, he said, 'Mr Sahil exact.'

Narses, who had been watching the exchange with an intent, but unreadable expression, now walked over with arms outstretched. 'Baabs,' he said to Isffy, 'I've missed you. Come here.'

Just then, the restaurant shook with the thunder of protestors outside.

Lunch with Narses, though a bland, disorganized affair, full of cellular interruptions, was important from our point of view for a few reasons. One: to have seen the expression on Narses's face when I brought up Mirwaiz's offer to drive me north. It happened like this.

He had said, unconvincingly, 'Abba is really looking

forward to spending some time with you. When were you thinking of going up to La Mirage?'

'I don't know,' I replied, draining the green drink to its icy dregs, 'I was thinking of just hanging out in Port bin Qasim for a while, then making my way up slowly. Your very charming driver offered to take me.'

'That's quite impossible,' Narses said, pale from the force of his reaction, his voice tight, 'your father would never allow it. The interior of our lovely country is now a dangerous place. It wasn't when I was a child; nor even when Isffy was a child . . .'

'You didn't know me when I was a child,' Isffy cut in, 'Shaista was still herself a child.'

'What difference does it make? What I'm saying is that it was safe till ten years ago, but is very risky now. It was stupid of Mirwaiz to suggest it. I must scold that boy.' Observing his reaction, I thought then that this was a nerve Isffy must never touch.

Narses, a conciliatory tone entering his voice, said, 'But why drive? Stay. Hang out. Soak up Port bin Qasim and when you're ready to leave, fly. It's a forty-five minute flight, you know. I hope you're finding the QC guest house comfortable? I did it up myself.'

'I haven't . . .' I began.

'Oh, yes, of course. You came straight from the

airport. Well, you'll see it after lunch. Be sure to tell me how you find it.'

'He won't be seeing it after lunch; he's staying with me,' Isffy said.

And now something else showed in Narses's face, something passionless and battle-ready, seeming not so much to hide emotion as threat. I knew too little then to understand what was behind it, but Isffy seemed to catch its every vibration.

As lunch ended, the manager reappeared with a young man. He wore grey shapeless trousers and a yellow checked shirt. He had a thick beard and small hard eyes, partially hidden behind the smudged and greasy lenses of his steel-rimmed glasses. At the centre of his dark fore-head was a thick grey callous with the texture of elephant skin. I recognized it immediately as a prayer mark, and was chilled to see so self-defacing a sign of piety in one so young. Mir Anwar, too, elegantly dressed, the manager of a fashionable restaurant, seemed embarrassed by his son's appearance. As for Narses and Isffy, a look of open disgust crept into their faces at the sight of him.

'You've raised a mullah, Mir Anwar,' Narses said, somewhat thunderously. 'Had I known, I might not have employed him at QC.'

Mir Anwar reddened, but tried to laugh it off. 'Sir, what can I tell you, this new generation, they have funny ideas. We were not like this. Of course we were good Muslims, but never so showy, sir.'

'What's your name, son?' Narses said, with the expression of a man confronted with a hideous deformity.

'Bilal,' the boy said, shrinking from their scrutiny.

'Bilal,' Narses said, as if committing the name to memory. 'Well, Bilal, let me look to see if there's an opening for a promotion. How long have you been working for us?'

'Sir, three years.'

Narses did not listen to his reply and looked away. When a second later he realized Bilal still stood there, he craned his neck around, and muttered, 'Well, good. We'll see what we can do. But . . .' And now he grew animated, as if all this time he had been working up his resolve. 'You'd do well to shave off, or at least trim, that beard a little. We're a modern company and Mr Tabassum does not like to see this overt show of religion in the workplace. Your religion is for your house; and it does not make you any less of a Muslim.' He spoke in a tone of upper-class authority that was at once assured and uncertain. I had heard it used many times in India, often by stern granddames with young men of religion;

there was an element of fear in it, as though they hoped, by the sheer force of their nerve, to quash a rebellion in its early stages.

The boy nodded and seemed about to reply, but thought better of it and simply nodded again.

When he had gone, relief passed over Narses's face. 'How awful,' he said, 'how awful. More than anything, how ugly. And in our own company! Mir Anwar, you know, was a Zeban-e-Pak man. That he should have raised this little fundoo. How awful!'

Then, as if wishing to shield the newcomer from these grim realities, Narses turned to me and said, 'Mummy wants you to come over to the house for Sunday crabs and beer.'

That evening – Saturday evening – once I had moved into Isffy's house, and we sat on black leather beanbags drinking beer, he said, 'He hates that you're a Tabassum, you see. And, forgive my saying it, a back-door one at that!'

The large room we sat in was like that of a child. Model aeroplanes hung from the ceilings; posters of racing cars, battleships and faded beauties – Turlington, Cindy Crawford and Evangelista – covered the walls; and, when the power failed, which was often, the room glowed with the ghostly green light of planets and stars from an Aerospace museum.

'What do you mean?' I said, and laughed. 'I thought he loved the Tabassums.'

'He loves my father. Our father, sorry. More than life itself, he loves him. But he hates the rest of us. He thinks it's unfair that people who have not proved their love should be close to the man he has worked so hard to be near.'

'Will he try to make trouble?'

'Only if he has the opportunity. And only if he feels threatened. You haven't come to Port bin Qasim eyeing the Tabassum millions. So what does he have to fear?'

In this I detected a note of warning from Isffy himself. I realized I was in eddying waters, full of cross-currents. But it didn't worry me too much: it was true I was not after the Tabassum millions. I had come to spend time with Isffy, to let the place wash over me, and to make my way north, in my own time, to La Mirage. My visits to my father's country in the past had been marked by the short, intense periods of seclusion I spent with his family. They had, I felt, been responsible for the raised expectations, and the big disappointments. I wanted now to enjoy my strange patrimony, with its many players and new country, to feel it more as an opportunity than an obligation.

Two empty beer bottles, the red labels drenched and peeling, stood on the thick glass of the coffee table. Eyeing them, my brother said, 'More beers?'

'Sure,' I replied. 'Do you want me to get them?'

'No, no,' Isffy said, with a smile, 'Zulfi! Beer aur laana!'

An assenting growl was heard from the well of the house, and soon the massive figure of Isffy's bodyguard appeared with two amber bottles.

'How come you need him?'

'Everyone does,' Isffy replied, pouring the beers into clear tumblers, 'there's a lot of kidnapping in PbQ, especially if your father's as rich as mine . . . ours is.'

Then, as if wanting to get something straight, he said, 'You know, Rehan, I met your mother once.'

'Really?' I asked, genuinely surprised. 'Where?'

'In Nepal, actually. Our father had taken my sister and me on a holiday there. On the plane, he got friendly with this nice woman in a purple and white polka-dot shirt — I remember that shirt so well — and when we landed in Kathmandu, he said that he'd made a friend who was going to join us on our trip. I remember that trip really well because it was just before he left my mother.'

'Oh,' I said, feeling in some inexplicable way guilty. 'And my mother?'

'That was her! She was the woman in the polka-dot shirt. I realize now that they would have had an arrangement beforehand, but this, at least, was how it was presented to us.'

'How can you be sure?'

'Bas, I'm sure. My sister remembers too.'

'Do you recall anything about her?'

'No, just the shirt and the big, seventies-style sunglasses. I hope you don't mind my saying this?'

'No, not at all.'

'Because you know, there's no issue. We're now both the sons of his ex-women, so what does it matter, right?'

'Right.'

'Then can I ask you one more thing?'

'Sure.'

'Why did you seek him out?'

I had a ready answer. 'Curiosity. Simple curiosity. My mother once warned me that he was present in my life as an absence, and that if I were only able to fix him in my mind, physically, that sense of absence would diminish.'

'But you did that.'

'Yes.'

'So what now?'

'Nothing now. I'm just seeing the thing through. And also, I feel a natural closeness to you guys . . .'

'Us guys?'

'The brothers and sisters. I half-suspected it might be that way, that I would make my connection to him through others, with whom there was less emotional baggage.'

He smiled. A quiet unreadable smile. Then he rose and opened the bay windows of his sweeping balcony. The moist night air came through the room. It brought with it again, as distinct as the night itself, the smell of the sea.

I inhaled it deeply, and said, 'It seems so close. Like it's not even a few blocks away. How far is it?'

'Just beyond,' Isffy replied distractedly. He seemed himself to have drifted off, as if his thoughts had become entangled in the night breeze. Then, as if aware again of my presence in the room, he said, 'Do you want to see a video I made?'

'Sure.'

He walked into another room, and returning a few minutes later with a silver laptop, came to sit next to me on the beanbag. He opened its screen to reveal an under-lit keyboard and a desktop cluttered with videos. Most of the video files bore the names of girls: Juggan, Maria, Aamina, ZQ. Sensing my eye pass over them, he said, by way of explanation, 'It's an obsession for me. I love seeing the red circle flash on the screen, the way the bland and familiar become interesting, and how even the dullest things can get this air of expectation about them. Ordinary shit, you know – a cigarette burning; a telephone; a shirt draped over a sofa; a panty; a mirror – seems so powerful. It's amazing.'

I had rarely heard Isffy speak with such feeling about any of his interests. Perhaps taking my silence to mean a lack of comprehension, he reached, without getting up, for the camera that lay on the coffee table, and whipping open its screen, showed me the room through its patient eye. Two or three lamps vied for space on the rectangular screen. Their light left a trail of white wandering fire, like that of burning magnesium. Isffy waited for it to settle, for the lens to adjust, then pushed his arm out. The room rushed by, like the headlights of a car plunging through a night fog. 'See what I mean?' he said and grinned. I didn't really, but was enjoying his enthusiasm too much to say anything.

Then the video came on and it was like nothing I had expected.

It contained none of his own camerawork, but was rather a collage of images from the 9/11 attacks. There were scenes of the planes, of people crying, of dust and fear. In the background, playing almost like an advertising jingle, was a song entitled, 'He's gonna get'ya, Osama'. It was a short, aimless exercise full of blue skies and fire, and it seemed the only theme as such was the palpable pleasure the filmmaker derived from the fear in the faces of the victims.

Isffy seemed to know that it could not be discussed. Indeed, when it was over, he put it away and turned his mind determinedly to what perhaps he had always intended to say. The video was like a way of alerting me to the trouble in his life, of giving me an oblique intimation of damage. And, appalled as I was by it, I felt it like a cry for help.

He rose, and in one movement, shut the laptop. He walked across the room to a sideboard on which there was a model of a Roman galley. He stood for a few moments with his back to me, playing with its little oars. My phone vibrated. As if collecting his thoughts, Isffy put the laptop carefully on the sideboard and turned around. 'I'm being blackmailed,' he said. 'I made a private video, a sex video, you can say, of me and this girl in the office; I stored it on my laptop; a foolish thing to do, I know, but it's fallen into the wrong hands and now I'm being blackmailed.'

It took an instant for his words to have their impact. I pulled my eyes away from the glowing screen of my phone, but my mind remained a moment longer on the contents of the message: one word from an unknown number: 'Mirwaiz.'

Aunty Christabel was Narses's mother. She was a frail half-German woman, who spoke English with an unusually strong subcontinental accent, as if to disguise her foreign blood. But she seemed to possess nothing of Narses's scheming nature, and Isffy had a special liking for her.

'If she knew what he was doing,' he said, on the way to their house that Sunday morning, 'she would break his legs.'

'Come on, Isffy. Are you certain it's him?'

'Hundred per cent. It's his style. He's always had this homo insecurity related to my father and me. This is just another version of what he's been doing to me since I was fourteen. Trust me. He doesn't want me to get married, you see. Because if I do, and produce the first Tabassum grandchild, it will seriously weaken his position vis-à-vis my father.'

Isffy was driving, filling the movement of the gears with the charge of his words. We drove through neighbour-hoods of honey-coloured bungalows with green and blue reflective glass windows. I had a strange wish for a land-mark, a square, a promenade, a monument, just something to help chart the grid-like sprawl. How nice the sea would be now! The glitter of its water to ease the little fevers that sprang up in my mind. But it didn't come.

'Who's the girl?'

'Her name is Mehreen, but everyone calls her Queenie. She works in marketing at QC. There's nothing too serious between us, but we've been fooling around for a while.'

'And the videos?'

'I always make them. It's a weird thing I have. Ever since I was fourteen . . .' then he broke off and smiled. 'I'm not sure I should be telling you this.'

I shrugged so as to say, 'Tell me if you want; don't tell me if you don't want to'; but really I wanted to know.

A Sunday morning quiet lay over the city; the streets were empty, and the sea-scented air seemed to whistle through the car's windows. I'd just drunk a coffee, and felt my senses sharp and awake. It was that distinct freshness of a first morning in a new place, when all your impressions have a mysterious power. Whatever the reason, I'll never forget the impact of Isffy's words, that cloudless day in a city whose shadows moved with the slow precision of a second hand.

'Ever since I was thirteen or fourteen,' he repeated, looking into the rear-view mirror, 'fucking chicks for the first time, it was not enough for it to be between just me and the girl. I needed another guy, a friend or a senior, to know, even to watch.' He paused, and glancing at me said, 'It was not that I needed this person to participate; I just needed them to be there, I needed them to see; without that, sex was not merely unsatisfactory or un-pleasurable, it was incomplete. As I grew up,' he added, 'I suppose the camera took the place of the friend.'

He had slowed the car down to say this, as if second, with its control and tightness, was the right gear for what he needed to express. And now he raced through third into fourth, with the impatience of a man suddenly embarrassed. But he needn't have been; I knew, as deeply as if the words had been stolen from the recesses of my own mind, what he meant. And what is more I knew the cause. I had also, from an experience with fathers – though, in my case, absent rather than wounding – known a need for male approval.

*

Narses was a different man that afternoon. At Aylanto, he had been guarded, full of hidden currents. But the person I saw, still lying in bed at one in the afternoon, was warm, open, round-cheeked and jaunty. An air of contentment pervaded his sunlit room. Everything was freshly painted, two large works of art by La Mirage artists, fresh out of their crates, sat awaiting a place in the house; a Labrador puppy bounded around the room amid a Sunday disarray of scattered newspapers. Narses himself was in loose blue shorts and a Tweety Bird T-shirt.

'Babs!' he said, greeting Isffy warmly. 'And Rehan baba! Welcome to my poor house. Please forgive the mess. Everyone has come at once, painters, guests, caterers, the art people. Tell me: what will you have to drink? Beer? I've just received a case of the most delicious Dutch beer. Dutch? Belgian perhaps. The crabs are on the way. You eat seafood, I hope, Rehan baba?'

I nodded.

'Oh good,' he said, and went off to find us our beers.

When he was gone, Isffy, his face full of distaste, said, with a mordant smile I recognized as my father's: 'Do you see? Do you see the signs?'

'No, of what?'

Isffy rapidly traced the shape of a heart in the air, and punching a hole through it, whispered noisily, 'Of love.

I am tormented for my relationships with women, forced to give them up, and this Narses is building a love nest for his little Kashmiri boy under my father's nose.'

I hadn't seen it that way myself, but it was the kind of assertion that whether true or untrue, once made, exerts an undue influence on the eye. I wanted to ask Isffy more about how Mirwaiz had ended up working for Narses, but my thought was cut short by the sound of raised voices upstairs. There was a shuffling of feet, the slamming of a door. We listened gravely, then heard a woman's voice yell, 'Narsu, come here this minute. I cannot take it a moment longer.'

When we reached the landing, Aunty Christabel was in great distress, sitting in a large chair with her eyes closed. She wore a red chiffon blouse and one hand was pressed up against her head while the other hung lifelessly. When Isffy approached, she opened her lidded eyes and raised her wrist.

Isffy took her hand, with its knobby-knuckles and thin blue veins, and said gently, 'What is it, Aunty?'

'Isffy, I've had it with that boy. He's going to be the death of me. They'll have to take out my *janaza*' – and this Urdu word for funeral was the only one she said with a foreign accent.

'Aunty!' Isffy said, laughing. 'What happened?'

'You don't know what he's been up to? The cook and bearer, men who've worked for me for over twenty years, since the Muree days, have just threatened to leave because of him. He's apparently been telling them that they must not call him Mirwaiz; they must refer to him as "sir" or "saab", if you please!'

Isffy, bending forward, looked under his arm and smiled at me.

'Sir or saab,' the old woman repeated, 'and do you know when I scolded him for it, not only did he not apologize, he stormed out of the house. This is all, by the way, Narsu's doing. He's spoilt the boy, taking him on trips and buying him shirts; it's all gone to his head. Narsu's problem is he's too generous; he doesn't understand that the person on the receiving end gets the wrong idea.'

Narses, in the meantime, had crept up.

'Oh, God,' he said, 'Mummy being melodramatic again. Has she fainted? Should I send for the smelling salts?'

'You might,' she said bitterly, 'but there'll be no one to get them. They've all left over the little Kashmiri viper you've bred in our midst.'

'Nonsense,' Narses said. 'Mirwaiz! Mirwaiz!'

'He's thrown a tantrum and left,' Aunty Christabel said, 'because . . .'

'Mummy . . .'

'Don't worry. I've already told them.'

The good humour fled Narses's face. Then he smiled benignly and rolled his eyes. It was a smile that was meant to accentuate the absurdity of the situation so as to dismiss it; it was a forgiving smile, forgiving of Mirwaiz's youthful folly; but most of all, it was meant to disguise the obvious tensions that had arisen in the house as a result of Mirwaiz's presence there.

'Come on,' he said, 'let's go sit in the other room. The crabs should be here any minute. Mummy will you have them served when they arrive?'

Aunty Christabel rose, gently wringing her wrists, and said, 'OK, OK, let's see if I can coax my staff back into good humour.'

Some twenty minutes later, Narses, Isffy and I were sitting at a glass dining table, in a bright room of floor-to-ceiling windows and garish art, when Mirwaiz returned. He had changed his clothes and there were some drops of water or sweat on his face. His handsome features, his intensely black eyes, his coppery skin and raised lips – features which until then I had only ever seen in the service of charm – now bore the cruel aspect I had thought them capable of when I had re-met him at the airport. He flitted around on the peripheries of the room while we ate, like a man wandering through a gallery. Narses tried to remain absorbed in his conversation with us, but his eyes followed Mirwaiz.

Abruptly, Mirwaiz stopped. And staring and pointing at something on the floor, he let out a loud, sadistic cackle. Narses looked up, then tried to ignore it, then couldn't and said, 'What is it, ja . . .' He stopped just short of using a term of endearment. Mirwaiz continued to laugh and point. His eyes shone with tears of amusement.

'The dog,' he said at last, catching his breath, 'the dog. Bozo. I didn't take him out when I should have and now he's taken a big shit on your new Persian carpet.' At this he bent over and laughed louder, a brazen, high-pitched laugh. 'And it's green! What have you been feeding him, Narsu?'

Narses paled. He looked to the side to make sure that his mother was not around. Seeing she wasn't, he hissed, 'Then why don't you pick . . . have someone . . .'

'Oh, what was that?' Mirwaiz said, his face bright with anticipation. 'Did I hear you correctly? You want me to start picking up dog shit now, is that right, Narsu?' Then suddenly the humour drained from his face, and he spat: 'Pick it up yourself.'

Narses looked at us with an expression that was like a plea for mercy. Rising, he walked over to where Mirwaiz stood and whispered something to him. There was a frantic exchange, which ended with Narses reaching out to touch Mirwaiz's arm. Mirwaiz pulled it away, hissing, 'Don't touch me.'

He marched in long strides towards the door, then abruptly stopped, and circling the table, came back over to where we sat. He leaned forward slightly, and whispering loud enough for everyone to hear, said: 'Isffy, Rehan, don't take it badly. Sometimes fights happen. You won't think me rude if I say that these people, not you both, of course, but the rest, are sick in the head. Take my word for it, Rehan baba, finish your business and get out. Otherwise, you'll end up like them. And you won't even know when the change happened.' He broke off, and with an odd tone of finality in his voice, added, 'Anyway, phir milenge. I still have your number.'

Then turning short on his heels, he strode out of the room with Narses trailing behind him.

After a few moments of silence, I said, looking at Isffy, 'It's worse than we imagined . . .'

'Better,' Isffy replied and smiled. 'Much better. This is the moment I've been waiting for.'

* * *

A week passed. The blackmailer's threats, of which there had been only a few until then, as if he himself was uncertain of the value of the video in his possession, became more frequent and intimate, delivered always via text message or email. The first that Isffy showed me had had a peculiar formality. 'Having sex video of you and Ms Mehreen, ma'am. Would be needing cash. Details forthcoming. Yours humbly, Masti ka Raja.' But as the days passed, the language of communication turned from English to a mixture of Urdu and English, dropping all vestiges of reserve and formality. Isffy, sitting in his office at QC, forwarded them to me.

I had fallen into an idle regime of whole afternoons spent on the leather beanbag, reading Russian novels and drinking nimbu panis. But every now and then, the flashing of my phone would disturb some bout of Dostoevskian frenzy.

'So, Mr Isffy, you like licking the phudi?' Or: 'Maro-ing Ms Mehreen, ma'am, in the bundh?' And that was the other curious thing about the messages. They seemed, more than a demand for money, to be an appeal for information, for sexual information. It seemed in some strange way that if only Isffy were to find the man, and sit him down and talk freely to him about all the things that animated his sexual curiosity, the matter would end there. He would hand back the tapes and go away, on perhaps the condition that Isffy would, from time to time, chat with him. There was also a note of confusion running through the blackmailer's messages, as though feelings of inadequacy and frustration in relation to women had been transformed into a kind of sexual admiration of Isffy – 'Oh, Mr Isffy, you really know how to give it to her, the doggy style. How big is your lundh?' It was almost as if, by his association with Isffy's, he, too, was hoping to become a man with a modern sex life.

It was clear from some of the information in the messages that the blackmailer was, in the broadest sense, part of the Qasimic Call family. Isffy was sure he was acting under orders from Narses, and even suspected Mirwaiz, pointing out that he was in and out of the house and could have copied the videos anytime. But I dismissed this possibility out of hand.

'Why are you so sure it's not him?' Isffy asked.

'It doesn't sound like him,' I said uncertainly. What I

really meant to say was that the blackmailer seemed too inexperienced, knew too little about life in general, to be Mirwaiz. And even from that brief acquaintance with him on the train, I felt this was too distasteful a business, too tawdry in its execution, to be conducted by someone like Mirwaiz.

But Isffy was not satisfied with this. To his mind, this was the newest version of an old game. Once again, the man who controlled his father, and foresaw the danger of Isffy producing an heir, had found a way of not simply disrupting the latest relationship in Isffy's life, but of discrediting him at the company that would one day form the largest part of his inheritance. He wanted to create a situation where it would be unacceptable for Isffy to enter a board meeting. And what better way to do that than to expose him as a man who exploits his power in the company for sexual purposes.

'You see,' he said to me, on one of the many balmy evenings we spent on Isffy's vast terrace, 'he knows that if I had a wife and children, our father, who wants in his heart of hearts to heal the rift between us, would be able to do it through them. He's in his mid-sixties now; he's slowing down; he wants to express the love he was never able to show me directly through people of my line. He sees that it is the only way to let me know that he wants it to be OK. But till those people, the linking people, are in place, he will rage, and continue to do harm to our relationship, because my presence, so long as I seem alone and unhappy, makes him feel guilty. And there's nothing our father hates more than to feel guilt. It is the one emotion that is as far away from his nature as is possible.'

'But this Mehreen girl, is she someone you might settle down with?'

'Maybe. At this point I don't need much. And she's very gentle and understanding. I just need to get her out of this Qasimic environment before Narses ruins my name at the company. I need to screw him first.'

'How?'

'Through this Mirwaiz business.' Once again I was about to ask him about the circumstances of his first meeting with Mirwaiz, wanting to hear his version of it, but he silenced me: 'I need a way to let my father know without making it seem that I am doing it to fuck Narses.'

I must have sighed at the dirty dealings of it all, for Isffy said: 'Don't get me wrong, bro. It's not by choice that I'm playing politics. I want out, too. But this guy, Narses, if I don't finish him, he'll finish me.'

'And you have a way of letting Abba know, without implicating yourself?'

'Yes, I think so,' he said brightly. 'I really think so.'

'How?'

'I'm not sure yet, but a few days ago, I received a message from Mir Anwar. Do you remember him?'

'The Aylanto manager?'

'Exactly. He's an old friend of Abba's, and though he kisses ass to Narses because he has to, he actually hates the guy. In his heart, he's an ally of mine, believes staunchly in the bloodline, the oldest son and all that crap, you know. Anyway, he sent me this message, saying he had some interesting info about Narses, info that he wanted to share with me, but said he couldn't do it over the phone. He says he'll tell me tomorrow in Marrakech at the Gym.'

'What's that?'

'A themed dance, one of the highlights of PbQ nightlife.' Then looking inexplicably at his watch, Isffy said, 'There's a Fifth Column meeting here first.'

'Fifth . . . ?'

'The show I'm producing. We'll go after that. You'll get a chance to meet some of my friends as well. And Queenie too.'

'She's coming?'

'Yes. And my pal, Momin; he's one of the great kings, or queens rather, of the Qasimic fashion scene. You'll love him.'

'And Anwar . . . ?'

Isffy looked blankly at me. Then leaning back in his chair and staring up at a naked bulb around which insects swarmed, he exclaimed, '*Mir* Anwar! He'll be at the Gym.'

'Isffy,' I asked, 'how come he's a friend of Abba's?'

'How come? What do you mean? He is.' Then gauging my meaning, Isffy explained, 'Don't be fooled by his appearance. He's not just the manager of Aylanto; he's the owner. It's just that he's a hands-on kind of guy. And big politically. He was in jail for a while under Gul. That's how Abba knows him.'

'Also a PPP man?'

'No, he's part of the Zeban-e-Pak.'

Seeing my vacant expression, Isffy explained, 'You remember the protest the other day?'

'The one against English?'

'Exactly. You saw how they caused all that damage on the rest of the street, but didn't touch Aylanto? That's because Mir Anwar is their guy.'

'What's the platform?'

'Linguistic purity. They're mostly immigrants from India who came here after the Partition, believing they were coming to a linguistic homeland, a place where Urdu would flower. When it didn't, when English became the language of the elite, they became disgruntled. They say, "The country was founded for a purpose; if it's not going to realize that purpose, then what is the point of the country?" That's our biggest problem, you know. Everyone has some high idea or the other about what the country was founded for, but it's always something completely divorced from the reality of the place, something we have to be and are not.'

'Isn't every place like that?'

'No. In other places, what you have on the ground becomes the foundation of your aspirations. Here, it's the other way round. There's always something abstract that needs to be imposed on the existing reality. And it fucks up everyone's moral compass. Because if you're always setting out to be something you're not, and are never going to be, if you're always chasing some Utopia or the other, then after a while you get fed up and stop bothering even to be what everyone is, which is human; your most basic morality starts to erode. And, Rehan, you know what they're about, these unobtainable Utopias?'

'What?'

'They're an excuse for retreat, for more nihilism and futility. Rumi says – though it could just as well be our founder speaking: "That which is not to be found is what I desire." So what do I do instead? I build high walls and retreat within them, I occupy myself with futilities. The Z-e-P, for instance, do you know what one of their central demands is?'

I shook my head.

'To convert all English books into the Nastaliq script!'

'To translate them?'

'No, no,' Isffy said, laughing now, 'to leave them in English, but to have all the English words, as they are, in the Urdu script. Now, if you're bothering to learn English in the first place, enough to read the damn books; not just this, but enough to be able to guess how English would operate in Nastaliq, to which it is obviously unsuited, then why not just learn the English script, which you probably already know?'

'How do they answer that?'

'They say that a language's spirit is in its script. And if you turn English into Nastaliq, you can conquer it once and for all.'

'But why conquer English? Why not just promote your own language?'

'Because English is power. But because you're afraid to admit that, you graft your own script over it, and sit happy with the illusion that you have conquered English.'

A little bewildered by all of this, I said, 'And do they have a large constituency?'

'Not so large, but energized. They're willing to die for their crazy ideas. And they're very powerful in PbQ. You touch one of their people, and you're a dead man.'

It could seem sometimes that for every man in Port bin Qasim – and there were fifteen million of them – there were groups and movements. There were green turbans, brown turbans and red turbans. There were six-inchers and twelve-inchers, depending on which relationship between piety and the length of your beard you believed in. There were purists, semi-purists and vernacularists, depending on which equation you struck between the purity of the faith and the purity of language. There were Shias and Sunnis, of course, but among them, too, there were innumerable divisions and sub-divisions. And these groups, each in their highly particular way, despised one another. They planted bombs at each other's meetings; they rioted at the slightest provocation; they dug themselves into breeze-block ghettoes that stretched for miles along the periphery of the city. To the outsider, especially if he fell in among the elite, who were irreligious and English-speaking, it was impossible to make sense of the divisions. It was as if men wished to distinguish themselves in the disorder that prevailed by fine-tuning their shriek every day to a higher and more particular pitch.

And, had so much violence not occurred as a result, had real blood not been spilt, their yearnings might almost have been mistaken for those of individuality.

These voices were to be heard, shrill and primordial, in Port bin Qasim's media, on its television channels and radio stations, in its newspapers. Every day new stories of exquisite and inscrutable rage emerged, but their cause never seemed equal to the intensity of their expression. And that perhaps was the point. The author of each episode, as though he were committing a kind of satirical suicide, seemed to take pleasure in the futility of his death.

There was, for instance, on the front page of the *Herald*, days after my arrival, a black and white picture of a self-immolation. The man appeared almost to be dancing as the white newsprint fire engulfed his body. It was difficult to know whether his expression was that of someone in pain or in the midst of an extreme euphoria. When I turned to the accompanying story, I read: 'Youth sets himself ablaze on discovering his name has Sanskritic origins.'

Or, a few days later, a wedding massacre in Sind. The pictures were awful: images of the young couple contrasted with scenes of butchery and chaos, the red and gold of a wedding lehnga stained with the deeper red of bridal blood. But once more, the motive for, in this case, fratricide was mystifying: the girl's brother and friends had turned on the wedding party with axes upon discovering that not a single member of the groom's side could convert simple Urdu nouns into their plural forms. *This*, from her brother: 'My suspicions were first aroused when I heard one of them say, "baz vakht". "Vakht?" I thought; strange that he didn't say "aukaat". So, out of interest, my friends and I, we began questioning them. And do you know what? Not one of them, not even the man who was to marry my sister, could tell me what the singular form of "auraak" was. Worse still, when we asked them to form agent nouns from simple nouns, "intezar" to "muntazir" say, not a man among them could do it. That was when my blood began to boil. I thought what kind of family am I letting my sister marry into? How would my nieces and nephews be raised? The shame! That was when my fury overcame me, and I took matters into my own hands.'

The makers of *The Fifth Column* expressed little interest in stories of this kind. As their parents had once been concerned with the British, they were now concerned with the Americans. And behind this concern, though ostensibly they wished to demonstrate the evils of 'the

American hand', lay a kind of love and admiration, not
unlike that of Isffy's blackmailer.

As I sat in on their meeting the following evening, I
realized that the video Isffy had shown me a week before
was not for private consumption at all, but was part of
many videos of this kind, and was intended for broadcast.

'We have to tell people what the white man is doing
in this region,' Momin said with great feeling, seeming, I
thought, to single me out for this statement of intent.
He was fat and effeminate, and dressed in a kaftan with
glasswork down the front. His skin was smooth and dark,
and his sloping eyes possessed something of the half-open
sagacity of the Buddha. Once he had made this declaration, in as energetic a tone as he could muster, and it
was met with thoughtful nods around the room, he lost
interest in the subject. He smiled and said slyly, 'But it's
quite nice to see how much we've been on the front page
of the *New York Times* lately, no?'

'For all the wrong reasons,' said the show's host from
one corner of the room. She was a pretty divorcee in her
thirties, with light auburn hair. Before she arrived, Isffy
had explained that she had once been married to an abu-
sive man. Apparently he'd called on her as a suitor one
morning. When he left, she consulted the Divan-e-Hafez
for guidance. She opened the book to a page that stressed

the importance of inner beauty. Aamina took this to mean that she should marry the man who had come to see her as he truly was very ugly. But he turned out, Isffy explained, to be 'a mean bastard: ugly inside and out'. So she divorced him and began life again. 'You don't just divorce in this country, if you're a woman,' Isffy explained. But Aamina did. She decided that religion was a purely personal thing. As part of her transformation, she began to wear Western clothes, found a job, and – this was straight from Isffy – got a nose job. Cosmetic surgery had become popular in Port bin Qasim and the town was filled with women still fresh from their surgeries, some still with little bandages on the bridges of their noses.

'But still,' Momin said, 'better than neglect, no?' His eyes twinkled, and his mind seemed to race. 'All publicity is good publicity.' A few titters went through the room. 'As Oscar Wilde, says, "The only thing worse than being talked about is not being talked about."' And now he seemed to receive the response he was accustomed to. The room rang with laughter, and Queenie, who had been sitting sulkily at one end of it until this point, said, 'Typical fag! Quoting Oscar Wilde.' She was dark-skinned and very pretty, with long tresses falling evenly over her breasts. Her face was lightly made up, her lips a little glossy.

At her provocation, Momin howled with laughter. 'Bitch,' he snapped. Then a story stirred in him. 'I've been seeing this guy,' he said, 'mawdel.'

'Butt-boy,' Isffy inserted.

'Hawt! Hawt, hawt, hot!' Momin said. 'Nineteen, with green eyes and dimples from here to here.' He described a line on his face, which stretched from his cheekbone to the small protrusion of a chin lost almost entirely on the smooth sloping expanse of his face. 'We'd fooled around a few times; nothing out of the ordinary; but then the other day I picked up this weird smell on him. I swear it wasn't there before. And I'd smelt him everywhere. The next time we hooked up it was there again. Finally, I said, "Listen, Kashif, I think you're hawt, but what is this smell? It's really not working for me." That's when he says he's using the new Marc Jacobs Cucumber. And it really smells of cucumber! *Kheera!*'

There were screams of laughter, and Momin, trying at once to finish his story and a cigarette, added breathlessly, 'I can't stand that smell. I said listen, "If you come tonight, you can't be smelling even one per cent of this stuff. I want a boy, not a salad!"'

The success of this last joke had the effect of adjourning the meeting for the night. The planners of *The Fifth Column* sent for more beers; Isffy pulled out a frozen bottle of vodka, which stood on a speaker, the frost on its surface turning to droplets; and soon, the group was agitating for the next phase of the night. Marrakech at the Gymkhana.

The club was an old British building set on many acres of darkened grounds. The heavy trees here and there had halogen lamps in their canopies, from which scraps of bright light fell on the well-mowed lawns below. The night air, alive with the competing and quarrelsome music of cicadas, was also infused with the scent of some nocturnal creeper, known variably from India to Spain as 'queen of the night' or 'dama de noche'. Past the club's white-pillared entrance billiard games were underway.

In a high-ceilinged room, with wooden beams, long-stemmed fans and hunting trophies on the walls, the players dived, crouched in stalking postures and sprang back again, in and out of shadow. Uniformed waiters, Scotch and sodas in hand, threaded their way past the vivid green expanse of the tables lit by low lamps. Against the sharp clicks and muffled thuds of the balls, there was the low murmur of men's voices. Women, not for Islamic reasons, but for old-fashioned colonial ones, were denied access to the great hall. Their distant laughter and the clatter of their heels was audible in the corridors encirc-

ling the room as they made their way to the wooden-
floored ballroom hosting Marrakech.

Once we had parted from the rest of the group, we
entered the billiard room. From the insulating light of
one of the tables, Mir Anwar's figure appeared. He had
been contemplating a shot when he saw us. He lost his
concentration and smiled brightly. I was taken aback by
how different he looked, now in his civilian clothes, and
expectant of service, rather than providing it. As we
approached, he whispered to his billiard partners, and
gingerly resting his cue against the table, picked up his
Scotch and soda. We met in the central aisle of the room,
through which there was a steady stream of traffic to and
from the club's deep verandas, where a mixed group of
men and women sat in rattan chairs.

The music of Marrakech was audible in the distance.
Indian film songs. Seeing it bring some enthusiasm to my
face, Isffy said, 'Do you want to carry on? I'll join you
inside in a few moments.'

'No,' I said, then caught in Mir Anwar's face the
special over-civility of a man who wishes to talk in
private. Neither wanting to go back on what I'd just said
nor to prevent them from speaking, I added, 'I'll stay for
a bit and then catch the action inside.'

'A lot of actresses,' Mir Anwar said with studied

suggestiveness. Then an expression of true sadness entered his face. 'I only wish,' he continued, 'that that silly boy, Bilal, would partake in this young people's fun. I keep telling him, "Go out, meet some friends, chat to some girls." But no: mosque, prayer, prayer, mosque, Koran. That's it. I say to him when I was young, we went out to dances, we learnt to twist and jive, we had girlfriends. It was all healthy fun. He tells me, "It's because of your generation that the country is in the state it is today. Unanchored, adrift, slaves of the West." Talk to him, Isffy. He's wasting his youth on this religious nonsense. It won't come back, you know.'

Isffy nodded thoughtfully.

Mir Anwar continued, 'And he's harming himself at the workplace. Your beloved uncle . . .'

'Not my beloved uncle.'

Both men laughed. 'Well, anyway, whatever he might be . . . the grand vizier . . . the Jafar . . .'

'The court eunuch!' Isffy said forcefully. 'In the book I'm reading, the Byzantine emperor has a parakoimome-nos, literally the eunuch who sleeps next door to him, and I thought that is what our Narsu is: Abba's parakoi-momenos. No?'

Mir Anwar laughed warmly. 'Good one, good one. I must remember that, para what?'

'Koi as in "koi hai"? And momenos, like momin and "os".'

'Koi-momenos,' Mir Anwar repeated. 'Anyway, what I was saying is that as long as he keeps that damn beard of his, the para-whatever is never going to let him rise in the office. And he's a smart boy. In fact, you know what I really think his problem is . . .' Mir Anwar dropped his voice to a whisper and Isffy leaned in.

But then Mir Anwar said loudly and clearly: 'He needs a good fuck. His problem is that he's twenty-nine and still a damn virgin.'

Isffy threw his head back and laughed. 'We'll arrange it, we'll arrange it. Not to worry, Meeru.'

Now feeling truly that more had been said in my presence than should have been, I rose to leave. Mir Anwar shook my hand energetically. 'Good to see you again, son. Come soon to Aylanto. All Tabassums are welcome.'

Isffy said, 'I'll see you inside, bro.'

I left them on the veranda. Isffy I was sure was about to do something stupid. It was written into his face, a childish transparency which I could see now must always have betrayed him. It was as if Isffy's rebellion against our father had stunted him, leaving him still a child at thirty-seven. But he was not playing with children, and entering the ballroom I had an awful fear of what he might do.

Inside, amid disco lights and the occasional strobe, were bellied men in bold shirts and women who hid their discomfort in Western clothes with the safety of black dresses. There was no bar, but waiters in fezzes carried steel trays between the tables. Some people danced in groups, in the manner of a middle school dance, but most stood around and watched. Occasionally, a big Bollywood hit song brought everyone to the floor, in a frenzy of raised arms and emphatic expressions. Then it would subside and the waiters would resume their activity. I had come around to one end of the room when I heard my name called in a long languid voice. I turned around and saw Queenie.

'So boring, no?' she said as I approached. 'I'm used to the clubs in Dubai, so this is so boring for me. I'm sure you know what I mean. I was saying to Isffy, "Let's just not go." I have a friend who has a hot tub on his roof. I said, "Let's go there instead. We can drink champagne in the hot tub." But Isffy didn't want to.'

'Why?'

'He said, "Port bin Qasim was itself a hot tub."' At this, she laughed loudly, then said sharply: 'I'm joking. Actually, he thought you would think it was cheap. Do you think hot tubs are cheap?'

'No,' I mumbled, trying to muffle my answer in the noise of the music.

But she wasn't really interested; she had something else on her mind. 'He cares for you a lot, you know,' she said, 'I've never seen him give a shit for anyone before. But he does for you, for some reason; I don't know why!' I began to see that this was her distinctive style; flirty provocations and confidences. Then looking deep into the crowd, she said, 'Look, Momin's found his gay-boy. Kheera-smell not bothering him too much now.' With this, she let out a peal of clear laughter.

Momin, aware of our eyes on him, looked over and trotted up. The boy melted into the crowd.

'Hawt, hawt, hot,' Momin said, as if pre-empting us, then added quickly, 'let's go out and have a fag.'

We followed him into a courtyard bordered with shallow stone steps. The tracery of backlit screens fell long over the floor. Momin sat down on one of the steps and leaned against a column. His face glistened with sweat, and he took the first few drags with the urgency of a man catching his breath. Then buttressing his voice with the casual authority of a smoker, he said, 'You know, I'm really glad you've come into Isffy's life.'

'That's just what I was saying!' Queenie interrupted, in a surprisingly energetic tone.

Momin nodded, as if to silence her. His eyes partially closed, the cigarette burned brightly. 'Because,' he continued, 'he needs an ally. It's been very tough for him. Narses, that bitch, has his father wrapped around his finger, and he's constantly trying to edge Isffy out, so that his sister, nieces and nephews can inherit everything. They've already cheated him out of the Flood Street flat . . .'

'What's that?' I said, finding its mention familiar.

'It's Sahil Tabassum's flat in London. They've put it in their name. They did it when Isffy and Sahil were on non-speaks. It's awful. And the father . . . your father . . . I hope you don't mind my speaking like this . . .'

I shook my head.

'. . . really screwed him up.'

He was quiet now, but it was only for dramatic effect. He wanted me to become more implicated in the confidence he was about to make.

I hesitated, then obliged him. 'How?'

Momin looked up at me from where he sat, his face cut in half by the shadow of an inward-sloping eave. 'Well,' he began, 'he seemed always to crush his self-confidence. And I think he was quite rough with him. Remember that in those days, ST was not a rich man himself. He was under a lot of pressure. In jail for fighting

Gul and what not. But I remember this one story Isffy's mother told me, which I never forgot. It made me very sad. Even now, telling it, dil bhar jata hai, the heart swells, you know?' At this, he looked at Queenie, who nodded in the gloom.

'This was when portable cassette players – do you remember them? – had just come onto the market. And Isffy, apparently, was dying for one; "obsessed" his mother said. He kept pleading with his parents to get him one, and they kept saying that it was too expensive. So Isffy started saving his pocket money; and he must have saved, I imagine, for a year at least. You know when you're a child, you get a few hundred roops a week. Max. But finally he had enough, and he goes out, without telling his parents, to buy one on the black market. Remember those electronics black markets that used to exist everywhere in the eighties?'

Both Queenie and I nodded.

Momin continued, 'Anyway, he buys the thing and brings it home, totally secretly. Listens to it for a few days, playing all his faves, Abba, Queen, and whatnot. Then forty-eight hours later, the damn thing conks out.'

Momin brought his face into the light, and taking a last deep drag, flicked the cigarette across the courtyard. Its embers scattered, and the little butt landed some distance away. Only the paper of its cylinder burned now.

'It was a fake-o, a dud!' Momin exclaimed. 'Isffy panicked. To lose a few thousand roops when you're a kid is no small thing. And in a moment of trust, he went to his father, and confessed everything. He must have been hoping that ST would help him catch the guy who'd sold it to him, or at least recover part of the money. Naturally this was not happening, but when you're a child you think your father can move mountains. So, anyway, he tells his father.

'And Sahil Tabassum, when he hears . . . Now remember, this is from Isffy's mother so it might be biased, but according to her, when ST hears, he not only does not console the boy, he starts thrashing him to within an inch of his life. Isffy's mother said she had to throw herself between the belt and her son because ST was beating him so hard, yelling all the time, "Useless, good-for-nothing, failure. Dope. Bozo. Idiot." All this to an eight- or nine-year-old child!

'No,' Momin said resolutely, as if alarmed by his own words, 'no doubt about it. Isffy's been through some tough shit. No doubt about it. When he was sixteen, ST, by then married again, packed him off to Eton. ST barely had the money, but he didn't scrimp on his son's education. The problem was that it was never for Isffy's sake; it was always done so that the son would add to the glory of the father. He sent Isffy to Eton so that he would make influential connections. Aristos: Bruftys and Buckys and Tollys, God knows who ST had in mind. But for one, England then was not what it is today. And two: Isffy was not the Maharaja of Jodhpur's son. He was a small Qasimic businessman's son, and people treated him like dirt. When he went back home for the holidays, he returned to his father's growing disappointment and a stepmother who wasn't much older than Isffy. So, yes, no doubt about it, Isffy has paid his dues. If, now, he's a little screwed up, fucking the women his father's fucked and filming it, I don't blame . . .'

'Momin!' Queenie suddenly burst in.

'Oh, God, I'm sorry,' Momin said, shaking with silent laughter.

There was no time for anything else, for Isffy had appeared at the far end of the courtyard.

He held up his hands in triumph.

'Fucked, fucked, fucked,' he said joyfully, and bounded up to us. His laughter carried across the court-yard, and was lost in the cavity above. I could hear the screech of his trainers against the stone; his voice rang out loud and hollow. A mobile phone gleamed in his hands, and he held it out as though challenging one of us to reach for it. He was sweaty and breathless. 'Go on, anyone.' For a moment, no one responded, then Momin stretched out his hand.

Light crept into the heavy lines and pulpy texture of his face. He remained expressionless as he read, until a smile of sly mischief animated his mouth.

'Jaani!' he said, guffawing lightly, his large mass beginning to tremble. 'It's too good,' he breathed, passing the phone quickly to Queenie. Her face was bathed in its white revealing glow. The polish of lipstick, foundation dust, the hollow shine of coloured contact lenses – all now became visible. She read a little more than Momin had: 'Mirwaiz, jaani, you know I love you.' Her laughter bubbled out of her. Isffy had joined the chorus, when at last the phone made its way to me. I read under the pressure of their reactions: *Why have you gone? I'm so upset. Mirwaiz, jaani, you know I love you. Please come back to me and I will make everything OK. Tonight.*

'But . . .'

'Scroll up,' Isffy said, 'and you'll see.'

I did; and seeing that the recipient – and now sender – was Mir Anwar, I realized what had happened: Mirwaiz, Mir Anwar. Such an easy mistake for agitated hands to make! And I could not help but think of the cruel indifference of the technology that had landed it in the wrong hands, and now, further exposed it before a hooting crowd.

'So then,' Isffy was saying, 'Narsu realizes what has happened and sends a second message to say, "Sorry for that, Mir Anwar; that earlier message was meant for my nephew." But obviously our Meeru had, by then, guessed the truth, and came running to tell me that he had some important info about our dear Narsu, info he could only share in person. But no sooner had we sat down just now than he forwarded me Narsu's message; I nearly fell out of my chair.'

'What did you tell him?' Momin asked.

Isffy feigned an expression of concern. 'I said, "You should go to Abba with this."' Then he choked with laughter.

The others howled. 'No! You didn't.'

'I did, I did,' Isffy said, 'I very much did. But what is more important is that *he* did.'

Introducing a kind of false earnestness into his voice, Isffy began, 'He wrote it in front of me: "Mian saab, I received this somewhat irregular message from Narses. I thought you should know about it. I cannot keep anything from you. He says it's for his nephew." And then he forwards him the whole message!'

'Oh my God,' Queenie said, 'he's quite a character, this Mir Anwar. I can't believe he could tell your father.'

'My father's ears, darling, are always open to informers,' Isffy said, 'even if they happen to be informing on the Head of Intelligence.'

Momin chuckled, and wetly clearing his throat, said, 'Then what?'

'Nothing,' Isffy exclaimed, widening the space between his fingers so as to create an air of mystery. 'For many minutes, absolutely nothing. We ordered a drink and sat down to wait. We finished it and ordered another, and still not a peep out of Abba. Then just five minutes ago, as I was getting up to leave, Meeru's phone beeps. A message from Abba. I can just fucking imagine him writing it. No explanation, nothing. All he says is: "Mirwaiz is the driver." That's all. "Mirwaiz is the driver." And you can just feel,' Isffy said, chopping his hand against his palm, 'the axe about to fall.'

* * *

I had not seen the sea in Port bin Qasim. In my last days there, it began to obsess me. I felt I needed it as a point of orientation, needed it to make real the possibility of escape. I had a dream one night that I was in a taxi, driving down the grid-like streets. The sun was at a tilt, setting I was sure on the water, but where was the water? I would stop passers-by to ask the way to the beach. They would each give elaborate directions and we would go further and further out of town. The city turned to cement shanties, all marks of municipality fell away; an early twilight prevailed and headlights swept past us. But there was no sign of the sea. And yet, its moist air, high with the smell of fish, seemed so near. I was sure it was only metres away. At last when the road turned to sand, I got out and began to run. But at every point when I was certain I would see its watery expanse, there was only deeper twilight and more sand. At last I could make out a figure in this wilderness. I knew it instantly to be Mirwaiz; but he was changed. His hair was all gone, his face gaunt and ashen. He smiled mockingly at me, but spoke with the same urgency with which he had told me on that first day that my father was the law. He now said, 'Rehan, there is no sea; there never was one; they made it up.'

Some particle, some seed of my dream must have pierced the veil of the next morning, for when I asked Isffy if I might take a cab into town, he said, 'There are no cabs. No cabs, no buses, no metro; unless you count the tempos, there is virtually no public transport. But take Zulfi.'

I found this, for some reason, almost as chilling as if there had been no sea. And that was when I realized that what I craved was public space. So not the sea then, but the beach, the promenade. I wanted to be near the chatter of people and the tread of feet; those things seemed to possess an inherent goodness in my mind while all that was private had acquired the fearful seclusion of secrets, cruelty and blackmail. Never at any time in my life had I trusted so completely to the morality of a crowd.

The scene at home had begun to turn uglier. Isffy's disclosure seemed to have had no effect and the black-mailer's threats redoubled. He spoke of having shared the video with people in the office, and Isffy, every day more paranoid, was certain he had received strange looks from his colleagues. The apparent failure of his revelation had drained Isffy of his taste for intrigue. He now sought a rougher justice. He spoke of his blackmailer with such violence, visualizing Mirwaiz or Narses, that I became concerned for their safety.

His rage was like the rage of a child, but fertilized, I feared very much, by an adult imagination. Anyone could be its recipient, anyone who Isffy might think of as having betrayed him. And this thought made me worry for myself, for I, too, had been nurturing a deceit. I was guilty of the greatest crime in both Isffy's and my book: abandonment.

On the night of Marrakech I had decided to cancel my trip north to see my father. The thought of spending time with him now was frightening. I had heard too much, and seen too vividly his imprint on Isffy for me to be able to meet him easily. I wanted to leave Port bin Qasim the way I came, by the Emirates flight. Not only this; by Tuesday of that week, I had chosen a day and booked and paid for a ticket. I was not sure why I had acted secretly, except out of guilt that I was betraying Isffy. At the same time, I knew that there would be no fixed day on which my brother's troubles would be over. They had come in cycles for over a decade and seemed no nearer their end.

I had mustered just enough courage to tell him I was leaving, but I had done it in an offhand, unspecific way, as if I was a wandering spirit who might hit the road at any moment. My time with him in Port bin Qasim had been marked by deep tenderness and affection. Affection that was expressed more through the merging of our routines than any outward declaration. And I could sense how much he enjoyed being in my company. He seemed to like to show me off. It gave him perhaps the double pleasure, of on one hand exposing my father's reputation to comment, on the other, of presenting himself as a man not totally without family.

And yet, I had not been able to tell him that our first Marrakech was to be our last, that some mixture of Port bin Qasim's repression and easy brutality had driven me away. It was the thing with places like this: their malaise – except for the bad moments, which, I sensed would be swift and violent, like a release – could feel like tranquillity. But the malaise was real and no sooner had I had an intimation of it than I was booked on the next flight out. Dubai that Friday at dawn; then, a few short hours in its purgatorial duty-free, and on to London.

With every passing day, I told myself that I would slip it into conversation, say something casual like, 'Isffy, bro, my time here is almost up.' But either the moment never came or the courage failed me. By Thursday afternoon, I had still revealed nothing of my plans.

That day, when Isffy was at work, I went with Zulfi to the Emirates city office on the pretext that I wanted to do some shopping. Now it would be easy, I thought. Isffy would come home in the evening, and I would tell him, as though I'd decided on a sudden whim, that I was leaving the next day, but would try to be back soon.

On the afternoon of my last day in Port bin Qasim, I thought often of Mirwaiz. Perhaps it was departure that made me think of arrival, and especially of that first arrival by rail, now five years ago. Or, maybe I was still toying with secret ways of getting to the airport at dawn.

The airline office stood in the shade of a large tree on a sloping Port bin Qasim artery. It was glass-fronted and air-conditioned, with a faded American Express sticker on the glass. Inside, yellowing pictures of metropolitan life in foreign cities were nailed to the ribbed wood-panelling on the walls. London scenes of Grenadiers and buses appeared alongside New York views of city lights and red skies, the towers still there, the Pan Am building still the Pan Am building. The pedestrians had eighties hairstyles, and the cars were of simpler colours, shapes and tyres. In one corner of the Sydney Opera House's blue sky, a scrawl in black pen: 'Rashid loves Ayesha'. The cool and shade of that office, with its window into the eighties, deepened my desire for flight. It made the world beyond not only seem far away, but of an another era altogether, as if in some time of riches the two had met, and since then, gone their separate ways. The yellowing pictures, unchanged over the years, and touched with a sense of longing, were like mementos of a ruined friendship.

I was leaning over the grimy surface of a thick glass table, under which brochures formed a collage of turquoise waters and inviting wildernesses, when my phone rang. The Emirates lady's red nails froze over the blue and red coupons, on which she pointed out my flight's routing and timing, PBQ, DUB, LHR. I wanted her to go on, but she wanted me to take the call. I was afraid it was Isffy, afraid that by some fraternal instinct he had guessed what I was doing; or, more simply, he had driven past and seen his car and bodyguard parked outside the Emirates office. I retrieved the phone from deep within a pocket.

Mirwaiz! The relief! Expecting to hear his voice, with its mocking note of abandon, it was some seconds before I realized that the person on the other end was not Mirwaiz at all, but a girl. A girl with a thin and frail voice, simpering almost; she pleaded with me to come quickly, she hadn't known who else to turn to; my name had been on his list of dialled numbers; yes, he had tried to hurt himself, but he was OK now; I was to come quickly; I was a Tabassum, I could help him somehow. He was too weak to talk, but he needed me; he said I was good and kind and would help; she was his sister. She had come down from La Mirage after the attempt. No, not a hospital; he had been discharged. They were in the Kala Gulab, in the inner city.

A few seconds later, my ticket in my pocket, I was back in the car, making jolting progress down the sloping avenue. Zulfi thrust the gears between second and third, ducked into side streets and flew past amber lights. The traffic screeched and honked at us, as Zulfi, by the sheer force of personality, broke lanes and zoomed up illegal openings, insinuating himself into the patient rows of traffic. When the city closed around us, its hardened arteries clotted with donkey-carts and rickshaws, he redoubled his pressure, and with a persistent, nudging movement, cleared the streets of their blockages. Not twenty minutes had passed before we were scanning rows of cheap hotels, their sleazy names projecting over the swelling street, searching for the Kala Gulab.

I saw it first. A slim cramped building, with a pink sign and red retroflective letters shimmering beside a bendy black rose. Like all the others, it had a dim tunnel of a mouth, doorless and black, opening onto the street. I told Zulfi to wait in the car and dived into it. With my eyes still adjusting to the sudden darkness, I caught hold of a flimsy banister and hauled myself up the stairs, stopping briefly on each landing to see the numbers on the doors. The corridors stank of disinfectant; on each level, a tinted transom gave onto the torrid street below, thick with traffic and brown smoke. On the third floor, I could just make out room number seven. I banged hard on the door and it gave way instantly to a tiny cubbyhole.

There was space for nothing save a single bed, a chair, and a white-plywood dresser on which lay deodorants, bottles of cologne, tweezers and a vivid bouquet of plastic lilies. Mirwaiz, I observed, even in this abyss of despair, had not forgotten his toiletries.

But for his hair, which was still long, he looked like the man from my dream. His cheeks were sunken; his temples had hollowed, the lips were thin and chapped; an unclean beard grew over the now deeper contours of his face. He lay on the white plywood bed and was covered up to his neck in a creased sheet. By his side sat his sister, who bore more likeness to the handsome man I had met on my arrival than the one now lying before me in the narrow bed.

When she saw me, she stood up, and bowing slightly, helped prop up her brother against the wall. He, in turn, looked briefly at her, and by way of re-introduction, said:

'The earthquake one, for whom I had gone to get the picture of the lake, remember?'

I nodded. He seemed even in his frail state to enjoy the attention, and smiled weakly at me, showing teeth over which a yellow film had collected. I thought he relished the expression on my face, when as he sat up, he revealed his two bandaged wrists, both wrapped in a thin white gauze, and daubed with two brown stains.

'Mirwaiz,' I said, 'shame on you. This is cowardice.'

His sister smiled encouragingly, and Mirwaiz, too, seeming to enjoy the rebuke, yielded to my words. 'What to do, saab? Life has been like that only. You don't know what I've been through. A harvest of troubles!'

'Giving lines?'

He laughed. 'Rehan saab, what lines are there with you?' Then becoming serious, he said, 'I'm telling you the truth. They threw me out like a dog. All the servants stood around me, saying, "Mirwaiz, sir, saab, where would you like your luggage to be taken? Where are you going from here? Of what service can we be to you?" Even that old bitch Narses's mother joined in. I felt like one of those princes, who are ejected forcibly from their kingdoms by a revolution. The swines!'

'Was Narses there?'

'No,' Mirwaiz said bitterly, 'where would that poor

wretch have been able to stand such a sight? As soon as word came from Sahil saab, his heart, or what remained of it, turned to ash. He handed over the responsibility of carrying out Sahil saab's order to his mother, and said, in a wavering voice, "Mirwaiz, I'm going to La Mirage on business. I'll be back in some three or four days. We'll meet then." But that of course was to be our last meeting.'

'Did you get any compensation or anything?'

'Yes, I did. But I was robbed of that too.'

'How?'

'The thing, Rehan saab, is this: when you remove an animal from his natural setting and rear him in a house, he loses his instincts. He ends up neither of the jungle nor of the house.'

Mirwaiz's sister, who'd been listening quietly up to that point, was so affected by these words that in a forceful mixture of Punjabi and Kashmiri she suddenly said: 'Truly, they've been savage with him. And it's not like we've had it easy.'

I nodded in agreement.

'If I hadn't come, God knows what would have become of him . . . I can't lose another family member; he's all I've got.'

'Speak in Urdu,' Mirwaiz interrupted.

But she fell silent, as if overpowered by her own words.

Mirwaiz, who had been listening with fascination to this account of his self-destruction, took over: 'The truth is that I lacked the courage to cut deep. I just needed to feel pain, physical pain, that could in some way cool my internal pain.'

As I sat there, listening to this tale of high drama, I wondered why I had been called here? Money? If so, I was happy to give him some. I had some dollars in my pocket, which I knew would go far in Port bin Qasim. Or was it something else they wanted? An appeal to Narses perhaps. That, I was far less willing to do. Help finding a job? But with whom? I knew only Tabassums.

For all his frailty, Mirwaiz followed my thought process at every turn. When reading my face, he could see it had reached a dead end, he said, 'Don't worry, Rehan saab, I want nothing from you. I want only to lighten my conscience. And yes, if by doing so, Isffy saab comes to feel that I am a good and loyal man, then I am ready this instant to come back into his employ.'

'Back into his employ?'

Mirwaiz eyed me carefully, seeming to weigh his options. Then he said, 'He hasn't told you who sent me to work at Mr Narses's . . .'

'Yes, but . . .'

'And *why*?'

As he witnessed the horrific impression his words made on me, Mirwaiz seemed almost to look with pity on my innocence.

'You were sent for that? To entrap Narses? Right from the beginning?'

Mirwaiz nodded solemnly.

'So what is the problem? Why didn't you go through with it?' I said, half in anger. 'Why do you need me to speak to him?'

'Because he's come to doubt my loyalty. I became soft, you see. I grew fond of Mr Narses, and could see he genuinely cared for me. I didn't want to betray him. And because of that Isffy saab came to think I was playing a double game. But I wasn't. I was always his man; I just couldn't do what he asked of me. And I want you now to help me prove my loyalty.'

The room became heavy with anticipation. The roar of the street was suddenly audible, the way a film's music sometimes takes the foreground.

'I know who it is,' Mirwaiz said at last, 'I know the man who is placing a price on the secrets of Isffy's saab's private life?'

A stylish way to describe blackmail, I thought.

But before I could know more, I needed to know something else: 'What, if any, connection does he have to Narses?'

'A distant connection,' Mirwaiz replied. A contorted smile creeping into his face, he added, 'This isn't Mr Narses's work. But let's say that if he was aware of it, he would not have stopped it either.'

I was very satisfied with this; it was just the kind of half-truth that was so well suited to Port bin Qasim. Mirwaiz, it seemed, had gauged the necessity for tact in the waters we found ourselves in.

'In my opinion then,' I said, 'there's no need to bring his name into any disclosure we might make.'

'No,' Mirwaiz said, letting his eyes rest on his sister. She had been watching in fascination, and now shook her head vigorously in agreement: 'No. No need at all,' she said.

Once more silence fell over the room; or at least we were muted, and the music of engines and horns played.

Mirwaiz pushed himself up higher against the wall, using the help of his turned-in wrists, and winced slightly from the pain. Our eyes followed him in expectation. Then, allowing a second to pass, he made an oblique gesture with his injured hand, indicating a flowing beard, rounded his fingers into a pair of spectacles, and rubbed his forehead with his thumb to suggest a prayer callous.

'Mir Anwar's swine son,' he muttered.

I returned to a bungalow enveloped in a dusk gloom. Isffy was not back and it seemed there were no servants about, for no one had switched on the lights. The chowkidar let me in, but even in his tired and lined face there were questions and anxiety; nothing, however, that he was prepared to put into words. He said only that Isffy saab was still out, and he had taken Zulfi with him. When I recalled Zulfi's ferocity, and the urgency with which Isffy had asked for him after I had shared Mirwaiz's information — 'Send Zulfi to me this minute, and wait for me at home' — that had a menace of its own.

It was like the mood of the house I entered, dark and tense, alive with the hum of a refrigerator. Silvery evening light, seeping into the front room from an invisible source, was dotted here and there with the red circle or icy blue square of a voltage stabilizer or air conditioner. I climbed the stairs, leaving the lower portion of the house to its darkness.

Upstairs, in the room where I had spent so much time, Isffy's glow-stars shone dully. I turned the knob of an uplighter and they vanished in the halogen glare. There were the relics of Isffy's childhood – the toys, leather beanbags and posters of plastic beauties. I thought I would take advantage of his absence to get my things together. When I'd revealed the identity of his blackmailer, I had also slipped in the news of my sudden departure. It had come so fast, and on so discordant a note, that he seemed not to register it at all. And yet, I wondered if he had felt it as another desertion. He had been so calm and collected, so businesslike in his manner, that I was not able to gauge his true reaction. He seemed once more the elder brother he had been on my arrival, once more the man in control, the man who had had my bags moved to his car without a thought. But where was he now? What had he meant when he said, 'If I'm late, go to bed and I'll wake you up when I get home'?

The hours passed and the quiet of the house deepened. Evening became night. I opened the bay windows in expectation of a breeze off the sea, in expectation of that balmy Port bin Qasim night, scented with brine, but it didn't come. What came instead was something thicker and velvety. A deep and sudden night, moonless. My suitcases were packed, but still open. Locks, money, my passport and ticket lay on the coffee table. There had been few times in my life when I felt so utterly without purpose. I dared not touch my Dostoevsky for fear of inviting troubled sleep. But neither did I want the glare and activity of the television. At last I sank into a beanbag, and began to wait, fighting my smarting eyes and drowsy mind.

I can't remember how I woke. But the house, which to its foundations had been asleep, was, like me, now awake to an uneven and jarring energy. A door slammed heavily; and the bungalow vibrated to it. There was also a phone ringing somewhere, an old-fashioned phone that I hadn't even known existed, a shrill landline. And beyond, a great murmur, as if thousands had collected in the street outside. I tried to process the different pressures logically. The phone. That was the first thing to find. I began hunting around and followed the ringing into Isffy's room, where I found it beneath a heap of unwashed clothes. Just as I lifted the receiver, I heard the sound of breaking glass in the room outside. And then the clarity of slogans, as if they had always been there: 'Khoon ka badla khoon se lenge/ We will avenge blood with blood.' And: 'Sahil Tabassum Murdabad! Sahil Tabassum Murdabad!/ Death to Sahil Tabassum! Death to his house!'

On the other end, Narses's voice: 'Rehan, is that you?

Thank God, I've got you on the phone. I've been trying for hours. Where's Isffy?'

'I don't know,' I said, doing my best to sound alert.

'Oh, God. Well, listen,' he sighed, 'we have to get you out of that bungalow. The entire Zeban-e-Pak is going to collect there any second, baying for blood.'

'Narses,' I said, allowing my ears to catch the dull clamour of voices outside, 'I think they're already here.'

There was a pause, then he said: 'Just wait there. I'm sending you an escort. I've spoken to the commissioner. Your father, poor man, has laid his turban at the feet of the Governor, begging for his son's life. It will be OK; just stay inside.'

'Narses,' I said, suddenly remembering, 'I have a flight in the morning.'

'Good. Very good. Where to? Somewhere far away, I hope.'

'Dubai and London.'

'Excellent.'

'Narses, what's happened?'

'Isffy,' he said with false calm in his voice, 'has tried once more to ruin us. That is what has happened. Such is his hatred for his family. Brutal what he did to that boy, Meeru's son. Unspeakable things. And he's not a nobody, you know; Meeru's got serious connections. But, you watch, he'll find out,' he added, his voice trembling with rage, 'he'll be the only one to suffer for this. He's only ruined himself.'

Just then, as if conjured up by this abuse, Isffy appeared in the doorway. His face was white and drenched with sweat. He put a finger to his lips.

'Rehan, are you there?' Narses said.

'Yes, yes,' I said.

'Well, sit tight. Someone will be there for you in the next hour or so. You are to leave the house from the servants' quarters. Understood? And if Isffy shows up, call me immediately.'

Isffy let the door close softly behind him. He was quiet. Outside a kind of orchestral violence reached its climax. Chants thundered and every now and then a pane shattered, drawing from the crowd a howl of euphoria.

'They have torches,' Isffy whispered with boyish excitement. 'Angry faces and torches, just as in olden days.'

'How did you get in, Isffy?'

'Through the back.'

He entered the room and sank to his haunches in front of an elaborate sound and video system, whose shape towered before us, like the darkened outline of a city.

With Isffy's touch, little red lights and pale green displays sprang to life on it.

'What are you doing?' I said, bewildered.

'Shhh,' he said. Then gently, turning a large black knob, he drew Begum Akhtar's voice, in a low whisky-ed moan, from the sound system. It filled the room, pushing back the commotion beyond.

Isffy stood up and went over to a little fridge, near the sound system, from which he drew two ice-cold beers. He handed me one and gestured to the bed. 'Sit down. I want to show you something.'

I moved reluctantly towards it. Isffy removed a small grey tape from his pocket, and fitting it into a VCR converter, slid it into the video player. Picking up the two remotes that lay beside it, he came to sit on the bed next to me.

The room was soon filled with the blue light that precedes the screening of a film. Isffy and I, cold beers in our hands, two thick feather pillows behind us, watched in silence. His face wore an expression of fatigue as deep as I had ever seen.

'We should have done this more often,' he said quietly.

I nodded, and for some reason asked if we would have to turn the music off.

'No,' he answered, 'it's not that kind of movie.' And grinning, he added: 'It's a silent movie.'

We sat like that for many minutes, the Begum Akhtar, soft and powerful, the room bright with blue light. Isffy's face was still pale, and his body damp with perspiration.

'You stink,' I said.

He nodded, and smiled thoughtfully, as if I had said something profound about our weeks together. A moment later, he said, 'I was very good and able once, Rehan. But I was wasted. And there is no anger like the anger over wasting what is good.'

I was about to say something. I wanted to tell him that I knew of the pressures upon him, knew, too, how these pressures no less than elemental ones could alter the moral composition of an individual. I wanted to tell him to resist, to remain what he was, what he intended to be. But what could I, who had resorted each time to flight in my own life, offer him? To stay, I felt now – no matter what you became – was to resist. And maybe it was better to be strong and corrupt than possess a morality that was not yours, that could only be adhered to through inaction and escape. In any event, I was too late.

Too late, for, like a director who has just introduced his film to his public, Isffy punched the button on the remote, and the still blue light of the screen was

extinguished by the sight of two black and white figures
in a deserted area. Isffy and Zulfi. The thin shadow of a
tripod fell long between them, fixing the time of day,
with the precision of a sundial, as late afternoon. Facing
them, as in an experimental theatre, was a single wicker
chair. At its feet a man sat slumped and half-naked in the
sand. Zulfi was tying his wrists to the hard wooden edges
of the chair. Isffy disappeared, then reappeared as shadow.
The camera began to move. It rested on an aerial view
of the half-naked man. His face was pressed sideways
against the plastic wicker; it was calm, as though com-
forted by the assurance of some greater justice. And even
in profile, it was clear, from the thick beard and spectacles, the pious patch of darkened skin on the forehead,
whose face it was.

Then the view swung up, and in the distance, molten
now in the sunlight, was the sea. No promenade, no
bathers, just a white abandoned beach, and for as far as
the camera's limited eye could perceive, the iron expanse
of the Arabian Sea.

Postscript

(London, July 2011)

A soft summer day. Rehan Tabassum looked upon it from the shade of a Notting Hill coffee shop with something like dread. Here, with the breadth of humanity around him, ethnic and various, flowing peacefully, it seemed, toward a certain end, the trouble in Port bin Qasim appeared to recede, appeared to be nothing more than a patch of turbulence on some distant tributary.

Rehan felt oppressed by the indifference of the great city, by its gentle rhythms and security, this sepulchral city, to which all the flights and tales of the world came. That both places could exist at once! And that he, Rehan Tabassum, should have to live in one while carrying within him, like an infection in his blood, the knowledge of the other. It was this that he found intolerable; it made him recoil from the pleasures of that summer day, from the diverse crowds, the ethnicities, the foreign films and newspapers — the world so near, it seemed, and its trouble so far, far from this coil of peace.

Opening his wireless options, he was assailed by a page-long list of choices. Hankypoo and Rubberducky stood out. He chose The Bean. And Googling 'Isphandiyar Tabassum' he was returned to those last days in Port bin Qasim.

In the end, it had been the bloggers who closed the circle, smashing the ceiling to let in the light. They spoke last, and in many voices:

It seems that the mystery behind Qasimic Call's slack service has been finally solved! According to this news report, the cable company's top executives MD Isphandiyar Tabassum and his bodyguard, Zulfikar, was arrested a few days back on charges of being involved in a porno case. . . . so much for broadband in port bin qasim!

Posted by Salman Siddiqui at 9/6/2011 12:22:00 PM

17 comments:

Anonymous said . . .

If Isphandiyar made a porn film with his girlfriend or shagbuddy then what is wrong with it? Why was Bilal nosy to first of all search for the clip (even if it was on laptop, not his task to open all movie files). Secondly even if he accidentally discovered it, why did he bother to brag about it and show it to other collegues. Talk about Isphandiyar and his girlfriend / shag's privacy. Or is it a crime in Pakistan to shag someone before marriage? lol you guys are so backward. tsk

16/6/11 7:04 PM

Anonymous said . . .

I dont think the issue here is who shagged who. Nothing justifies illegally imprisoning someone, strippin them naked, sodomizin them and makin a movie of the whole crime-the magnitude of the crime reported in the Herald is horrendous. It's a criminal act and the perpetrators deserve severe punishment.period. it's awfully sick when people try to justify other people's crime. but no worries, the present status quo in the country guarentees that the perpetrators will walk scot free. I'm sure papa Sahil Tabassum will dish out some from his many many millions to save his skin . . . let's all say Pakistan Paindabad once more shall we? -anonymous II

17/6/11 3:25 AM

Anonymous said . . .

I agree with you. He should be punished but he wont
be. But dont forget that the Bilal guy should be
legally charged as well for invasion of Isphandiyar's
privacy. It is not the petty Bilal's business to snoop
around his boss's system for secrets and then have a
laugh at it with other employees. His actions
provoked Isffy, and the flipside is that Isffy is
powerful and can get away with it so he screwed his
life up. thanks

19/6/11 5:33 PM

Anonymous said . . .

Pakistan Paindabad!

19/6/11 11:39 PM

Anonymous said . . .

did it ever occur to anyone that bilal might be lying
in his version of events. and the Herald is famous for
sensationalism, so i wouldn't really beleive everything
reported. maybe it's time to question what anyone

ANY one would do if they found out their dirty linen had been strewn all over.

20/6/11 4:40 PM

Anonymous said . . .

If i could then i would do the same as Isffy did. It is not about dirty linen. I am shagging my girl and making its video and we both consent to it. Nobody has the right to see it without our permission let alone stealing from our computer and showing it to the rest of organisation. Bilal is the asshole in the picture anyway you look at it.

22/6/11 4:26 PM

Aqeel said . . .

You did removed my comments, I know the reason ;) You are a pure patriot Pakistani, a real Paki Lover, who says 'sab say pahly Pakistan and the Pure Language'. So that's why the freedom of speech is not allowed in your constitution. Feeling very sad :-(about our country and people . . .

22/6/11 9:37 PM

Anonymous said . . .

Pakistan a country of corrupt, jealous, callous and psuedo-patriots. No freedom whatsoever unless your daddy is in Army or is a Fedual lord or is a big industrialist. I spit on a double standard society / country like that.

23/6/11 4:04 PM

Anonymous said . . .

shutup asshole . . .

1/7/11 3:06 PM

Anonymous said . . .

For the life of me I dont understand if ISffy wanted to set an example, for god's sake, he should hve used the Guard to butt-fuck the dude . . . but nooooo . . . Mr. MD had to get a taste of the anus himself . . . One stupid person.

7/7/11 12:23 AM

Anonymous said . . .

Where can we get Isphandiyar's video?

8/7/11 9:51 PM

port bin qasim said . . .

hi . . . wish I'd found this page earlier. anyhow, nothing wrong with making a video but how stupid to leave it on an unprotected laptop in a media company! even more stupid to dip into the company ink . . . Queenie, the girl sat across his office, some ex-kgs marketing chick . . . no wonder they get so many adds for their channels!!!

13/7/11 3:35 AM

port bin qasim said . . .

who wants the video?!

13/7/11 3:00 PM

Anonymous said . . .

please place the link of th video here..for public good!

15/7/11 3:38 PM

ruhollah said . . .

you guys are sick. Why are you surprised at Bilal's snoopin if all you want to do is watch yourselves?

I can see now what the end of our porr country will look like: 'nasty, brutish and short,' like a bad student film.

18/7/11 3:40 PM

Anonymous said . . .

Brutish maybe, but definitely not short. This is feature-length, baby. Countries don't 'end,' they just rot away slowly

20/7/11 3:48 PM

ruhollah said . . .

but the violence, does anyone know where it has come from? did we know it was there?